"Hannah..." Her heart pinged at the concern in his eyes. "Are you okay?"

The low, intimate sound of Laurent's voice almost undid her. Memory after memory rushed through her brain. How he used to leave her voice mails that made her blush and giggle. His mouth against her ear when they would be out with others, whispering a compliment, a promise. The Saturday mornings when they used to cycle to their favorite French bakery in Putney Heath and eat breakfast while playfully flirting, her legs trembling when his fingers would stroke her hand, her arm, her cheek, before he would suggest that they head home. His murmured words when they made love afterward that had swelled in her heart and burst like joyful bubbles in her bloodstream.

Hannah breathed in deeply. She was over him. She had to remember that fact.

Dear Reader,

A few years ago I vacationed in Bordeaux and in the nearby Charente-Maritime region. I was blown away with the beauty of both the city and the countryside—think magnificent châteaux, picture-perfect villages, historic cognac houses and gentle rolling hills of endless vineyards. Inspired by the region and in particular by the fairy-tale-pretty châteaux I knew I had to write a wedding story featuring a gorgeous French best man and base it in the picturesque town of Cognac.

I adore second-chance stories. They hold so much poignancy and heartache. So I created my two characters to be ex-lovers whose relationship ended when it became apparent that they held very different views on marriage—Hannah McGinley, my reserved, cautious but ever-so-brave heroine and wedding celebrant, and Laurent Bonneval, my charismatic cognac house CEO and marriage-skeptic best man, who guards his heart ferociously for fear of giving another person the power to hurt him.

I hope you find this book with its central theme of owning and respecting our feelings an uplifting read and that you enjoy escaping to the beauty and tranquility of this very special but sometimes overlooked region of France.

Happy reading!

Katrina

Second Chance with the Best Man

Katrina Cudmore

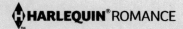
HARLEQUIN®ROMANCE

Recycling programs
for this product may
not exist in your area.

ISBN-13: 978-1-335-49941-7

Second Chance with the Best Man

First North American publication 2019

Copyright © 2019 by Katrina Cudmore

Printed in U.S.A.

A city-loving book addict, peony obsessive **Katrina Cudmore** lives in Cork, Ireland, with her husband, four active children and a very daft dog. A psychology graduate with an MSc in human resources, Katrina spent many years working in multinational companies and can't believe she is lucky enough now to have a job that involves daydreaming about love and handsome men! You can visit Katrina at katrinacudmore.com.

Books by Katrina Cudmore

Harlequin Romance

Romantic Getaways

Her First-Date Honeymoon

Swept into the Rich Man's World
The Best Man's Guarded Heart
Their Baby Surprise
Tempted by Her Greek Tycoon
Christmas with the Duke
Resisting the Italian Single Dad

Visit the Author Profile page at Harlequin.com.

To Majella, the best little sister in the world!

Praise for
Katrina Cudmore

"Poignant, uplifting and impossible to resist...*The Best Man's Guarded Heart* is the perfect book to lose yourself in on a lazy afternoon.... [S]killfully balances humor and warmth with pathos and powerful drama leaving the reader on the edge of her seat and eager to find out what happens next."

—*Goodreads*

CHAPTER ONE

THE BEAST PRESSED his snout against Hannah McGinley's car window, the glass instantly fogging up. 'Good doggy, off you go, now,' Hannah called out, trying to sound in control but also cheerful—the last thing she wanted to do was anger this beast any further. Her arrival on the driveway of Château Bonneval had already caused him to run alongside her car like an entry at the Grand National, his incessant barking almost causing her to drive into one of the hornbeam trees lining the long avenue.

As a farmer's daughter from Shropshire, she'd been told time and time again she'd no cause to be so scared, but no amount of cajoling from her family had ever rid her of her terror of even the smallest of dogs, never mind the donkey-sized version staring at her right now as though he couldn't wait to sink his teeth into her.

Looking in the direction of the front door of the château, Hannah willed someone to come out and rescue her. Surely they had heard the beast's hound-from-hell baying?

Not for the first time, Hannah wondered at her decision to agree to travel to France to act as the celebrant at her best friend Lara's wedding blessing. An easy, joyful decision in most circumstances, but not when you had dated and fallen in love with the best man and brother to the groom, Laurent Bonneval, only for him to end it all. And the worst part of it all was that the wedding was taking place in his home—Château Bonneval. Why couldn't it at least be at a neutral venue? Her only hope was that they would be surrounded by others all weekend and she would manage to project the air of calm professionalism she'd been rehearsing ever since Lara and François had travelled to London from Manchester, where they lived, just to ask her to be their wedding celebrant.

Though moved beyond words that they trusted her to perform their wedding blessing, especially given the fact that she was so new to being a celebrant—this would only be her fourth wedding—she'd asked if they were really, *really* sure it was she they wanted to be the one to perform the ceremony. Lara and François had exchanged a tentative glance before Lara had leant across the table of Hannah's local Richmond coffee shop, and touched her arm. 'You've been my best friend since we were seven.' Pausing, Lara had given her a half-smile, one that had asked Hannah to understand, to trust her. 'It would make our day even more magical to have you bless our marriage.'

Tears had blinded Hannah for a moment as she'd remembered how Lara had waded in on her first day at Meadlead Primary School and told Ellie Marshall and her gang to mind their own business when they had interrogated Hannah during the break with endless questions as to who she was, why she was joining the school in the middle of term, why she was so skinny. Frozen inside, confused by everything in her life, Hannah had been taken aback at just how grateful she was to Lara when she'd led her away from her interrogators. For weeks after, she'd remained silent. And while that had garnered her endless suspicious glances and whispered words behind cupped hands from the rest of class, Lara had cheerfully chatted away, her quirky humour and buoyant outlook on life thawing Hannah's numb heart.

That day in the café in Richmond, Hannah had turned to François, her heart as usual jolting in remembrance—some of François's features were so like Laurent's: the thick dark wavy hair, the strong and proud Gallic jawline, the wide, high cheekbones, the clean blade of a nose.

'Will...?' She tried to form the word Laurent, but it stuck in her throat and refused to budge. Eventually she managed to mutter, through a false smile, 'Will having me as the celebrant be okay with all of your family?'

François's eyes were different, a softer, more forgiving blue, none of the striking, pain-inducing brilliance of Laurent's. The care in his eyes had matched his gentle tone when he had answered, 'Laurent is to be my best man,' but Hannah had still felt it like a whip to her heart.

She'd looked away from the discomfort in both Lara's and François's expressions, hating that they had been put in this position. Their wedding should be a carefree celebration, not tainted by the fact that she'd foolishly fallen in love with Laurent, confusing his Gallic charm and romantic gestures for a sign that he'd felt what she did, that he too had wanted more.

In the months after he'd left London to return to the family business and château in Cognac, telling her before he left that he didn't want to continue their relationship, she'd puzzled over the overwhelming effect he'd had on her. The pain, the disappointment, the humiliation had been so engulfing she'd struggled to comprehend it all. Was it the fact that he was the first man she'd ever truly fallen in love with? Which admittedly was pretty tragic at the age of twenty-nine. But up until then, she'd never met anyone who had quickened her heart, who had communicated so much with a glance, who intrigued her.

At first she'd resisted the chemistry between them, her age-old need to protect herself holding him at arm's length. But in truth she'd been changing and had been more receptive to allowing someone into her life. She'd chased security and stability throughout her early twenties, desperately needing the safety of establishing her career in finance and buying her own apartment. But as she neared thirty, she'd realised she wanted more. A more free life, a more optimistic life. One of taking chances and not being so afraid. And into this new way of thinking and daring to dream had walked Laurent Bonneval. The brother of her best friend's new boyfriend. And he'd swept her off her feet. But ten months later he'd left her with a broken heart.

But that heart was now mended and firmly closed to Laurent Bonneval's charms.

Hannah jumped as the beast's tail hit against her door panel as he turned and bounded away, disappearing around one of the château's fairy-tale turrets that sat at each corner of the four-storey building.

She breathed out a sigh of relief. But then her heart plummeted to the car floor. From around the corner, sprinting at first, slowing to a jog when he took in her car, came Laurent, the beast at his side.

Stopping, he raised a hand to shield his eyes from the low evening sun. Behind him his shadow spilt across the gravelled drive, his tall, broad frame exaggerated.

She waited for him to move. Tried not to stare at the fact that he was wearing only running shorts that revealed the long length of his powerful legs and a lightweight vest top that showcased the taut, muscular power of his broad shoulders and gym-honed arms. His skin glistened with perspiration.

Heat formed in her belly.

He moved towards her car.

Her heart somersaulted.

She grasped for the window control and buzzed down her window a couple of inches, only then realising how stifling the car had become as she'd been held hostage by the beast. She longed to run a hand through her hair, check her make-up in the mirror. But she resisted giving him any sign that she cared how she looked in his eyes.

He came to a stop a few feet away from the car. The beast came to heel at his command. 'Hannah...' Her heart pinged at the concern in his eyes. 'Are you okay?'

The low, intimate sound of his voice almost undid her. Memory after memory rushed through her brain—how he used to leave her voicemails that had her blush and giggle. His mouth against her ear when they would be out with others, whispering a compliment, a promise. The Saturday mornings when they used to cycle to their favourite French bakery in Putney Heath and eat breakfast while playfully flirting, her legs trembling when his fingers would stroke her hand, her arm, her cheek, before he would suggest that they head home. His murmured words when they made love afterwards that had swelled in her heart and burst like joyful bubbles in her bloodstream.

Hannah breathed in deeply. She was over him. She had to remember that fact. Her focus now was on deciding which direction her life should take. Stay in her career in finance either in London or Singapore or take the risk of becoming a full-time wedding celebrant in Spain. Her old cautious side told her to hold on to her regular income and secure career but deep inside of her she wanted to be free to make her own decisions away from the confines of corporate life, to make a difference by being an integral part of one of the most important days in any person's life.

She was here to support Lara. To celebrate

with her and François. Laurent Bonneval was just a minor aggravation in what should be a gloriously happy weekend.

Now was the time to enact the calm professionalism she'd sworn she would adopt for the weekend. Unfortunately her trembling hands and somersaulting stomach didn't appear to have received that particular memo.

She buzzed down her window a fraction more. Nodded in the direction of the beast. 'I'd appreciate it if you'd lock him away.'

Something unyielding kicked in Laurent's chest at the coolness of Hannah's tone and stony expression. He pointed in the direction of the stables; at his command Bleu ambled away to where he slept alongside the horses.

Hannah's gaze followed Bleu's every step and even when he disappeared from view, her gaze remained fixed in that direction. 'Will he come back?'

He edged closer to her door, crouched over to speak to her in the small gap of the window. 'I heard him barking—I'm sorry if he scared you.'

She shook her head as though to deny any suggestion she'd been scared. 'Is he yours?'

'Yes.'

She grimaced at that. He knew that she was scared of dogs. He cursed himself for not having locked Bleu away. Lara had told him Hannah was due to arrive around this time but Bleu had looked so despondent when he'd led him to his kennel earlier, Laurent had relented and allowed him to accompany him as usual on his evening run. 'Despite appearances, he's as soft as a marshmallow. He just wanted to say hello to you.'

Hannah shook her head, clearly not believing him. 'He's terrifying—I've never seen anything like him.'

'He's a Grand Bleu de Gascogne. He has a very affectionate temperament.' Moving to the car door, he opened it. Hannah's gaze shot back to the corner of the château where Bleu had disappeared and then back to him. He gave her a smile of encouragement. 'He won't come back, I promise. You can trust me on that.'

Her forehead bunched and her mouth dropped into an even deeper scowl.

For long seconds she stared at him unhappily, heat appearing on her high cheekbones, but then with a toss of her head she yanked her handbag off the passenger seat and stepped out of the car.

In the silence that followed he cursed François. When François had told him that Hannah was to be their wedding celebrant he'd been incredulous. François knew of their history, how uncomfortable it would be for them both, but François, usually so sanguine, had refused to change his mind in the face of Laurent's demand that someone else take on the role. His only compromise was his pledge that he and Lara would be present in the château at all times over the weekend to smooth any awkwardness between him and Hannah.

'Your journey—was it okay?'

Hannah shrugged at his question and moved to the boot of her car. 'I'd like to go inside and see Lara.'

By her tone, he knew she was as keen as he was for the others to be present in the château. But once again, his father had decided to make life difficult for everyone around him. He followed her to the boot of the car and lifted out her suitcase. 'François and Lara called me earlier—there's been a change of plans. They're now staying in the family apartment in Bordeaux overnight. Lara tried calling you but she couldn't get through.'

Her expression appalled, Hannah pulled her phone from her handbag, 'I'm having problems connecting to the French network.' Then with an exasperated breath she asked, 'Why are they staying in Bordeaux?'

'Apparently my father had already made a restaurant booking for them and refuses to cancel. He wants to show Lara and her parents some of the city's nightlife.'

Her head turning in the direction of the château, she asked uneasily, 'So who's staying here tonight?'

'Just you and me.'

Her eyes widened with horror.

Irritation flared inside him. He'd known she wouldn't be keen for his company, but did she have to make it so obvious?

But then his indignation sank into guilt. He and he alone was the cause of all this tension. The least he could do was try to make this weekend somewhat tolerable for them both.

Leading her in the direction of the main entrance, he said, 'Let me show you to your room. All of the château staff have this evening off as they will be working long hours in the coming days with the wedding.' Inside the coolness of the double-height hallway of the château, his desperation to take a shower and have something cool to drink abated a fraction. The heatwave hitting most of south-west France for the past week was becoming unbearable. He kicked the front door shut with his heel, knowing he was only trying to kid himself—the weather had little to do with how he was overheating.

This always happened when Hannah was nearby.

Pale pink sleeveless blouse tucked into mid-thigh-length lemon shorts, plain white plimsolls on her feet, thick and glossy brown hair tied back into a high ponytail, she was all delicious curves and sweetness.

He uttered a low curse to himself. He knew he'd hurt her. She deserved better than him remembering how incredible it was to hold her, to feel her soft curves. But in truth, their relationship had been built on a bed of intoxicating mutual attraction.

He'd seen it flare in her eyes in the moments after they had first met, their handshake lasting a few seconds longer than necessary, neither trying to pull away.

That first day, as they'd sailed on his yacht, *Sirocco*, which had then been moored out of Port Solent but was now moored out of Royan, Hannah had been friendly but he could tell that she was avoiding being alone with him. He'd wanted to shrug off her indifference but in truth her reticence had intrigued him and the intelligence in her eyes and her close friendship with Lara had had him wanting to know her better.

She had turned down his invitation to meet for a drink later in the week.

So he'd orchestrated it for her to attend a dinner party he'd thrown in his Kensington town house. He'd hoped to impress her with his cooking but she'd left early, saying she had an early flight to Paris in the morning. As he'd walked her out to her awaiting taxi, for the first time ever, he'd felt tongue-tied. All night he'd been unable to stop staring across the table at her, her natural warmth that was evident behind her initially reserved nature, her genuineness, her authenticity lighting something inside him. On the few occasions she had looked in his direction, he'd seen that spark of attraction again, but she'd always snatched her gaze away. That night of the dinner party, he'd let her go, without pressing his lips to her cheek as he'd ached to, something deep inside him telling him he had to wait until she was ready to accept the spark between them.

Their paths had crossed several times in the months that had followed. He'd used to playfully remind her that his offer of meeting for a drink was still on the table but she would smile and turn away.

And then, one day, when they had all gone swimming in the Solent after another day sailing on his yacht, *Sirocco*, she'd watched him dive from the rail. When he'd emerged from the water deliberately close to her, her initial frown that had spoken of some deep internal turmoil had transformed into a gentle smile and she'd softly said, 'I think I'm ready for that drink.'

He'd trod the cold English Channel water, grinning widely, not caring that everyone else in the party could see his delight. He'd wanted to stay there for ever, staring into Hannah's soulful brown eyes, his heart beating wildly in delight and anticipation that had been more than about the desire to tug her gorgeous bikini-clad body towards him.

Now he led her up the main marble staircase of the château to the second floor where, at the end of the corridor, he opened the door to her bedroom. Hannah walked inside, her gaze widening as she took in the antique jade hand-painted wallpaper, the Louis XV furniture.

He stayed at the doorway. They had dated for over ten months. The chemistry and intense attraction never waning, escalating in fact. But as they'd grown closer, as his heart had begun to need her, panic had set in. Laurent didn't believe in love and commitment. When he'd been twelve, François ten, his father had left the family home to conduct an affair. The following year his mother had done the same. And in the years that had followed his father had disappeared from the family home at least once a year to continue his affairs. The affairs, the hurt they had inflicted on everyone around them, had poisoned Laurent for ever against any thought of commitment in his own life.

His panic had soared when he'd visited Hannah's family one weekend and seen their love and devotion to one another. How could he ever bring her into the toxic mix of his own family, which was so full of unspoken anger and accusations? And his panic had soared even more when Hannah had told him of her plans to become a wedding celebrant. At first he'd laughed, thinking she was joking. But she'd been serious. The woman he'd thought of as being as career-minded and as focused on success as he was, who had never given any indication that she was looking for commitment, wanted to be the officiator of the institution he'd no regard for—marriage.

Increasingly he'd realised just how incompatible they were despite their attraction and laughter and warmth for one another. And then he'd learnt of his father's stroke and his need to return to Cognac to head up the family business. For years he'd waited on the sidelines to be given the role of CEO, beyond frustrated at the decline in the Cognac House's market share under his father's neglectful leadership. Bonneval Cognac had been in existence since the seventeenth century. It was Laurent's legacy and one he was determined to restore to its rightful place as the most exclusive cognac house in the world. It was a promise he'd made to his beloved grandfather before he died, a man who had despaired at his own son's disloyalty and irresponsibility, not only with the business, but with his own family.

Knowing that there was no future for him and Hannah, Laurent had ended their relationship when he'd returned to France. It had been a gut-wrenching conversation, and he'd seen the pain and confusion in her eyes, but it was not a conversation he regretted. Hannah deserved someone who actually believed in love and commitment. Someone who reflected the love and devotion and stability of her own background.

This weekend would be awkward. But they needed to somehow build a new relationship as their paths would cross time and time again in the future. Maybe having to spend time together this evening was an opportune time to begin that process. He was the one who had messed up by allowing their relationship to become too intense—the least he could do was ensure that the next few days were as painless as possible. For both of their sakes.

'I had planned on eating out tonight—I need to go and check on my wedding present to François and Lara first, but there's a restaurant nearby. Will you join me?'

CHAPTER TWO

Hannah studied Laurent and marvelled at his ability to forget the past. It hurt her, angered her, but part of her envied him for it. Wasn't it what she was striving to achieve herself, after all? For a moment she was about to say no to his invite. The last thing she wanted to do was spend time alone with him.

Standing in the doorway, a shoulder propped against the frame, his arms crossed on his chest, his expression untroubled, he waited for her response. He was still the best-looking man she'd ever met. And damn it, she was still attracted to him. As her mum would say, *figgity, figgity, fig*. Well, if he could shrug off the past then so could she. She popped her suitcase on the luggage rack. Flipped the lid open, pulled out her laptop and placed it on the desk by the window, determined to have some control.

Opening up the laptop, she asked him for the Wi-Fi password and, logging in, she said, 'I'm doing an online thirty-day yoga challenge and I want to do today's session now. I'll need a shower afterwards.' She glanced behind her in his direction. 'I won't be ready for at least an hour so don't wait for me if that doesn't suit you.'

'I didn't know you practised yoga.'

She shrugged. 'It helps me to let go of all those small things that irritate me in life.'

He made a grunting sound low in his throat before saying, 'I'll see you downstairs in an hour,' and then walked away.

She closed the door and leant heavily against it. This room, the entire château, was beyond incredible. She'd stolen glances into the endless rooms they had passed downstairs, her breath catching at their delicate elegance.

It was hard to comprehend that Laurent lived here. All alone. She knew from Lara that his parents had moved to a lodge on the thousand-acre estate after he'd returned from England to take up the role of CEO. She'd heard Lara's description of this magnificent château, had known of the world-famous cognac brand, but until now she hadn't fully grasped his family's wealth and standing.

This was not her world. It brought out all the inadequacies she so desperately tried to keep hidden.

Now, more than ever, she was glad that she'd never told Laurent about her early childhood. How could someone who came from this background ever understand her? Not believe she was tainted by it?

She was even more grateful that she'd never fully opened her heart to him, dared to tell him she loved him. She'd felt too vulnerable, too unsure of what his response would be—which should have told her everything she needed to know about their relationship. Though deeply charismatic, Laurent somehow managed to never fully reveal himself or show any vulnerability. For most of their whirlwind relationship she'd been blind to that, too excited by the fact that this gorgeous man wanted her in his life. He'd been attentive and fun with a determined and self-possessed streak she'd found utterly compelling. But he'd never really answered her questions about his background, what he wanted in the future. And in their last conversation he'd told her that he couldn't give her commitment, a permanent relationship.

Thankfully she'd managed to stop herself from pleading that she was happy to keep things casual, knowing that in truth she only wanted to buy more time to persuade him that he could commit. At least she hadn't followed that particular deluded path of trying to change another person.

After her yoga and shower, she changed into a knee-length white shift dress, a narrow gold belt cinching in the waist. Brushing out her hair, she let it hang loose and applied some make-up. About to leave, she paused to stare out of one of the four windows in the room. Below her room, set amidst a wide purple border of lavender, sat a huge swimming pool. Beyond the pool an immaculate lawn ran down to a tree-lined river. Laurent used to talk about that river, the Charente, when he spoke about home, which admittedly was a rare occurrence. In London, his whole focus had seemed to be on his career as a fund manager and the busy social life he'd created in his adopted city. He'd lived life with abandon, hungry to experience new places, new things—she'd travelled more in her short time with him than she'd ever previously done.

Downstairs she busied herself with staring at the landscape paintings of country scenes hanging in abundance in the hallway as she waited for him, and when his footsteps tapped, tapped, tapped on the marble stairs as he jogged downwards, she realised how much she missed his endless energy and enthusiasm for life. She gave him the briefest of smiles when he came alongside her, tried to ignore how good he looked with his damp hair, his pale blue shirt open at the neck worn over lightweight navy trousers, tried to ignore how his freshly applied aftershave flipped her heart with the memory of waking to find him crouched beside her, dressed for work, a cup of tea in one hand, a plate with toast in the other, his brilliant smile turning her weak with happiness.

'Ready to go?'

She nodded to his question and followed him to the front door. As he was about to pull the ancient handle that opened one side of the heavy double oak doors she could not help but ask, 'Will he be out there?'

He turned, confused at first by her question, but then reached out as though to touch her forearm. Hannah jerked back, unable to bear the thought of him touching her. Afraid for how she would react. For the briefest of moments he looked thrown by her reaction before he dropped his hand. Opening the door, he answered, 'No. Bleu knows to stay in his kennel when I send him there.'

Tentatively she followed him out onto the gravelled driveway. 'Did you inherit him from your parents?'

He walked to the side of the château, past a parked four-by-four, and opened the doors of one of the five stone-crafted single-storey out-buildings that were set back from the château. Daylight flooded the building to reveal a silver sports car. Hannah swallowed the temptation to exclaim at its beauty.

'I didn't inherit Bleu but this car I did inherit. My father is an avid vintage-car collector. He moved most of his collection to an outbuilding at the lodge but left this car here as there wasn't enough room for it. He wanted to sell it but my mother persuaded him to keep it within the family. I don't get to use it as much as I'd like to…' he paused and glanced out at the blue, cloudless evening sky '…but this evening is the perfect night to take it for a run.'

Hannah watched him manually lower the soft top of the car, the pit of disappointment in her stomach at his answer having her eventually ask, 'So where did you get Bleu?'

In the initial days and weeks after Laurent had returned to France she'd held out vain hope that he might call, change his mind, her heart slowly splintering apart, but after a month of silence, her heart a void, she'd accepted that it was truly over between them. But somehow, the thought of Laurent choosing Bleu, knowing her fear of dogs, spoke more than a year of silence of him moving on from her.

After he'd left she'd been numb, but eventually, when she'd grown exhausted by the emptiness inside herself, she'd insisted that her heart mend. She'd worked harder at fixing her heart than at anything she'd ever tackled before. She had thrown herself into her work and her training course to become a wedding celebrant. She'd filled every minute of every day with work and exercise and reading and meeting up with friends and family.

Only once had she slipped up and shown just how deeply devastated she was. She'd taken her newly acquired wedding celebrant certificate to show to her parents on the day she graduated from her course. Her dad had been out at the weekly livestock market in their local town, but her mum had made a fuss of her achievement, even opening a celebratory bottle of champagne. In the comforting cocoon of her childhood home, once the euphoria of achieving the qualification had worn off, she'd realised how tired and lonely she really was. And when her mum, with her usual gentle perceptiveness, had asked how she was, the tears had come. Hannah had fought their spilling onto her cheek, not wanting to upset her mum. She'd just nodded instead at what her mum said in response to her hiccupped short explanation before quickly changing the subject to a much happier topic—her sister Cora's pregnancy and the much-anticipated arrival of the first grandchild into the family.

Later, back in London and alone in her apartment, she'd reflected on what her mum had said and taken some solace from her observation that at least she was risking her heart now and living life as she should be, with its invariable ups and downs, joy and disappointments. Hannah had been taken aback; she hadn't realised that her mum saw through how much she was protecting herself. Which was silly really—her parents were the most empathetic people she knew. Of course they understood why she struggled so much to trust others.

She'd met her parents when she was seven. She hadn't wanted to be in their house; she hadn't wanted their smiles, their kind voices. Their encouragement to eat her food, to play with their daughters, Cora and Emily. She had wanted to be back in her old house. With her birth parents. But the police had taken her away and now she had to live with new people. She'd been so scared. Above all else she'd hated change. Because it meant things might get even worse. She'd known how her birth parents operated, but not these strangers.

Now opening the passenger door for her, Laurent moved to the other side of the car. It was only when they were both seated inside the car that he turned and answered her question. 'I found Bleu one night when out running in the woods of the estate. I heard his whimpering first—the vet believes he ate some poison a local farmer may have put down. He was already an undernourished stray. We didn't think he'd pull through. But he did. He's a gentle giant. But I'll make sure he's locked away while you're here.'

Hannah swallowed at the tenderness of his tone, at the emotion in his eyes. Torn between her deep fear of dogs and the guilt of locking away this poor animal who had been through so much already, she answered, 'No, don't, that's not fair on him. I'll keep out of his way.'

Turning on the engine, which started with a low throb, he turned and regarded her. 'I can introduce him to you if you want.'

She jerked in her seat, instantly terrified. 'No, don't.'

He gave her a concerned look before backing the car out of the garage. When he'd turned it in the direction of the drive he said, 'You never really explained to me why you're so scared of dogs.'

She shrugged. 'I've always been petrified of them, it's just one of those things.' Which wasn't true. She could remember a time when she wasn't scared. But like so much of her early childhood, the story of why she feared dogs was one she'd locked away inside herself years ago.

Laurent's gaze narrowed. For a moment he looked as though he was going to probe further but then, putting the car in gear, he sped off down the drive and out onto the narrow lanes of the Cognac countryside.

The wind whipped against her hair. She tied it back with an elastic band from her handbag. Despite her anxiousness about the entire weekend, for a moment she felt exhilarated as they zipped along and she smiled to herself as the force of the warm air blasted against her skin. The car was small. Laurent's thigh was only inches away from hers. She tried to focus on the low hedges they sped by, the endless bright fields of smiling sunflowers, the gorgeous order of vineyards with their row upon row of vines, and not the way Laurent's large hands clasped the wheel, the assured way he handled the car. They slowed behind a tractor. Hannah felt a jolt of nostalgia for her Shropshire childhood. The rides with her dad out on his tractor. The carefree days filled with her dad's laughter, the late evenings of drawing in bales of hay. But even then a part of her could not help wonder how she'd managed to escape from what came before, wondering if one day she'd have to go back to it.

Laurent slowed as they approached a village. The road narrowed even further to wind its way past pale stone houses with light blue shutters, then a *boulangerie* shut for the evening, a bar with some locals sitting outside who waved to Laurent as he passed by. At the other end of the village he pulled into a narrow driveway, a plaque with the name Villa Marchand on the entrance pillar, the viburnum hedging dense with white delicate flowers brushing lightly against the sides of the car. And then a two-storey house appeared, its blue shutters tied back. Jasmine and wild roses threaded their way up the outer walls, curling around the Juliet balconies on the upper floor. To the side of the house stood an ancient weeping willow tree on the banks of a river.

Laurent parked the car and got out. Hannah followed him to the front door. He opened it to reveal a stone-flagged sitting room, large white sofas surrounding a heavy teak chest that acted as a coffee table. The walls were painted in a soft white; a large grey painted mirror hung over the open fireplace.

'Why are we here?'

He frowned at her question as though he'd expected her to already know the answer. And then, stepping into the room, he said, 'This is my present to François and Lara. A summer home. It's where François proposed to Lara. I'm hoping it will tempt them to visit more often.'

She followed him into the room, leaving the front door ajar. 'You miss François?'

He turned at her question. Her heart lodged in her throat as his blue eyes twinkled and his wide generous mouth lifted in a smile. 'Don't tell him.'

Before she could stop herself she heard herself say, 'You could always move back to England to be closer to him.'

She turned away from how his expression fell, winced when he said, 'My life is here now. I'll never leave Cognac again.'

Picking up a small bronze figurine of a cat from the side table, she said, 'That's quite a turnaround from before.' She lifted her gaze to study him. 'You used to say that there was nothing here for you.'

'Things change.'

'But not people. They just reveal their true selves to you.'

'I never—'

Regretting instantly the bitterness of her voice, that she'd revealed her upset with him, Hannah interrupted with a forced laugh, 'You're certainly putting my wedding present of a set of organic cotton bath towels into the shade with this villa.'

Laurent shook his head. 'The infamous wedding list.' Pausing, he gave a smile. 'It has caused a lot of amusement amongst my parents' friends.'

Hannah swallowed a giggle, imagining the other guests' bewilderment at some of the items Lara and François had listed. 'I think water filters, recycled furniture and garden equipment for their allotment are very practical gifts to ask for.'

Laurent's eyebrow lifted. 'My father had to explain to a friend of his who's a guest at the wedding what a wormery is. Trust me, it was a very long telephone conversation.'

Hannah smiled, trying so hard to pretend that she was finding all this easy, a bittersweet thickness forming in her throat at how easily they fell back into their shared humour and banter.

Silence fell between them. Laurent's smile receded. The room closed in around them. She looked away from him. But even then she felt the force of his gaze. Heat grew on her cheeks, a rumble of attraction stirred in her stomach and, when she glanced back at him, it exploded at the rigidity of his expression—his square jawline fixed, his dark thick brows drawn downwards, his mouth stern. She'd at first been drawn to his easy charm but it was this

more private, serious-minded side of him—
the responsible older brother who was so protective of his only sibling—this self-assured
and professionally astute man she'd fallen in
love with.

His jaw moved a fraction. The chemistry that
had always been so strong, so potent between
them was at work again.

She willed herself to walk away, to break the
silence, regretting having come here.

His mouth tightened. The knot of fear and anticipation twisted even tighter in her stomach.

'How have things been for you?'

She jolted in surprise at his question. His
voice, as always, like warm honey trickling
through her insides. For a moment she was
about to answer in a similarly low intimate
tone, but caught herself in time and instead,
with a flourish of bonhomie that took even her
by surprise, she walked away, pretending to in-
spect the books in the bookcase. 'Great. I've
been busy. Emily married late last autumn in
Granada in Spain. We had a great week there—
it really is a beautiful city and it was so nice for
all of my family to have spent the time together.'
Her forced smile was replaced by a genuine one
when she added, 'And Cora had a little girl.
She's called Diana. She's gorgeous. I'm totally
smitten by her.'

Laurent smiled at her description. For the briefest moment, the old ease that had existed between them flared. Hannah was thrown; her smile faded, and disappeared altogether when she thought of her sisters' happiness. She loved her sisters with all her heart and would never begrudge them anything…but faced with how content they were, how successfully they managed their personal lives, Hannah not only felt lonely but also doubted she would ever manage to achieve a similar happiness.

Laurent winced as the wistfulness in Hannah's expression was replaced with an unsettling sadness. She wanted what her sisters had. Marriage, children, a united family. The things he could never give to her.

He gestured for her to follow him into the kitchen, a sudden urge to keep moving, to be distracted by doing things, taking hold. 'Let me show you around. I had an interior designer manage the renovations and furnish the rooms but I could use your advice as to whether there are additional items Lara would like.'

Hannah walked around the island unit of the hand-painted kitchen, her gaze shifting out onto the garden and the river beyond. 'Have they seen the villa since you redecorated?'

Earlier, when she'd asked why they were here,

for a moment he'd been thrown by the fact that she didn't know. Somehow it felt as though she should know everything that was happening in his life. 'Not since their last visit. They had wanted to stay here before the wedding day but I told François that there was a problem with the electricity.'

'When are you going to tell them?'

'I'll give them the key on their wedding day. They can spend their first night here together.'

The weariness in her expression faded and the warmth he'd so adored about her in London appeared. She gestured around her, towards the kitchen and then the garden outside. 'Lara is going to be so happy. She has always wanted a garden of her own. Right now they only have their allotment and that's miles away from their apartment.' In this enthusiasm, her happiness for her friend, he realised how much he'd missed her. He missed this warmth, her laughter, her sheer presence.

Pointing towards a notebook hanging from the kitchen's noticeboard, he said, 'Take a look upstairs and note down anything you think I should get the interior designer to add.' Then, backing towards the garden door that led out onto the newly laid patio, he added, 'I need to check out some work that was carried out in the garden today.'

Outside, he walked across the stone patio—
as he'd guessed, the contractor had done a good
job—hating his need to get away from Hannah.
From her smile. Hating the reality of what he'd
walked away from.

He was standing on the riverside steps when
she came out and joined him ten minutes later,
handing him a bullet-point list in her neat and
precise handwriting. She'd listed bathrobes,
champagne, Belgian chocolates, decaffeinated
coffee and a double hammock. He lifted an eyebrow at that last item.

Hannah laughed and gestured towards the
giant willow. 'It'd be fun for them if it was hung
from the willow across to the boundary trees. I
can see them lying there on their wedding night
staring up at the stars before going to bed.' Her
voice trailed off and her gaze dropped down to
the new wooden rowing boat that he'd asked his
interior designer to organise.

Heat radiated from the stone of the river steps.
There was a vague creaking noise as the over-
heated house and earth shifted in expansion.
But the heat on Hannah's cheeks, the heat in
his belly, had nothing to do with the weather
and everything to do with her mention of bed. In
London, they would meet after work sometimes
in the city, other times he would meet Hannah
off her train in Richmond if he'd been travelling

that day, with the intention of having a drink or a meal, a visit to the theatre, but more often than not they would head directly home and into bed and only surface hours later to eat before tumbling back into bed until the following morning.

Hannah had always craved chocolate after they had made love. She had a particular love for dark chocolate straight from the fridge. 'Do you still have an addiction to chocolate?'

Her head whipped around at his question, a spark of anger in her eyes. 'I try to stay away from things that aren't good for me these days.'

He forced himself to smile, knowing he deserved that comment.

She folded her arms, stared across the river towards the bank of poplars growing there. She bit her lip for a moment and paused in deep thought before saying, 'Now I know what's missing in the house—I couldn't put my finger on it for a while—family photographs. You should get some framed and placed around the house to add a personal touch. I can send you some of Lara and her family.' She paused and considered him. 'You don't think it's a good idea?'

He rubbed the back of his neck and admitted, 'I can't remember the last time my family had a photo taken together.'

She grimaced. 'Not with your dad being ill and everything.'

He didn't bother to tell her that it was probably close to a decade since they'd had a family photograph taken. In the years after he'd left home, Laurent had rarely returned to Château Bonneval, and when he had his visits had always been brief. Some briefer than others when he would leave almost immediately, completely frustrated when his father would refuse to listen to his advice on saving the business.

He walked down the steps and, pulling the boat towards himself, stepped into its hull and turned to Hannah. 'Let's go for dinner. The restaurant is a ten-minute row down the river.'

Hannah stepped back on the grassy verge and considered him. As she tilted her head to the side her ponytail swept against her shoulder, exposing the arched curve of her neck, and a memory of her giggling when he used to press his body to her back, place his lips on the tender skin of her neck, left him momentarily dizzy. The boat rocked beneath him. He jerked, almost losing his balance.

Hannah laughed. He shook his head at her amusement at his predicament and almost lost his balance again.

When she joined him on board she sat down

as clumsily as possible, obviously in the hope of tipping him into the river.

Laurent effortlessly rowed against the light flow of the water and Hannah studied the neighbouring gardens they passed by, seeing in the long and narrow plots the unfurling of family life. A woman on a recliner reading a newspaper while her husband clipped a bay tree. A family of five sitting at the edge of the river eating dinner beneath a huge oak tree and stopping to wave hello as they passed by. Hannah wanted this domesticity but would it ever happen for her?

A surge of anger towards Laurent caught her by surprise. Why had he come into her life? Why, when she'd lowered her defences for the first time ever, thereby allowing herself to fall for a man, had he broken her heart? And as she watched him pull on the oars, his shirtsleeves rolled up, his forearm muscles bunching with each pull, her anger soared even more. She didn't want to be so aware of him, so giddy around him, so vulnerable, and her resolve that she would never let him get to her again hardened.

She needed to remember his faults. He liked to eat strong-smelling cheeses that had made her gag whenever she'd opened his fridge. He took work even more seriously than she did—how often had he cancelled dates or forgotten about them, to her annoyance? And despite his gregarious personality, in truth he was a closed book. She knew so little about his background, his family. And he had a birthmark on his bottom. Okay, so she'd admit that that was actually cute.

'You're starting to scare me.'

She jumped at his voice. 'What do you mean?'

'You look like you're trying to figure out the most effective way of murdering me. In fact, it reminds me of the evening your work colleagues came to a party in my house.'

Their first fight. 'You were over an hour late for your own party. My colleagues were wondering if you were a figment of my imagination.'

His eyes glinted. 'Ah, so, despite your denials to the contrary, you had been talking to them about me as I had suspected.'

I couldn't stop talking about you. I could see my colleagues' amusement as I recounted things you had said and done, day after day, but I was too giddy with amazement over you to stop. 'They wanted to see for themselves if your wine collection was as impressive as I said it was.' She smiled when she admitted, 'My senior partner especially. He was rather put out when he saw it was a much more extensive collection than his.'

And then she remembered what had happened that night after the others had left, how Laurent had made love to her in the moonlight that had streamed through the window and onto the floor of his bedroom, his eyes ablaze with passion and emotion.

She dropped her head. Inhaled against the disturbing mix of desire and pain that was grabbing her heart.

'How's work?'

She looked up at his softly spoken question. Had he guessed she was remembering that night on his bedroom floor? Her anger resurged. 'I've been offered a promotion which would involve a transfer to the Singapore office.'

Up ahead on a bend in the river, below a string of lights threaded through trees, a wooden sign on the riverbank announced that they had arrived at La Belle Epoque.

Laurent guided the boat towards the restaurant's river steps, nodding approvingly to her news. 'That's fantastic. When are you moving?'

He shifted the oars inside the boat, wood upon wood making a solid thump, a sound just like the thud her heart gave to his enthusiastic congratulations.

She gritted her teeth and eyed him, not caring at the hurt heat flaming in her cheeks. Did he not even feel a single pang that she would be moving so far away? How could he not realise how torn she was about leaving her family behind?

The move to Singapore was an incredible opportunity, but in truth, deep down, she was scared of being lonely...forgotten by her family.

'Are you going to accept?'

She shrugged at his question. 'Do you think I should?'

He considered her for a moment and then those blue eyes blazed with an ominous energy. 'Is something or somebody keeping you in London?'

She folded her arms. 'Perhaps.'

The blaze in his eyes intensified. 'Are you dating someone?'

She'd been on some dates during the past few months; wasn't getting back on the figurative horse the best way to get over a fall? By dating other guys she'd hoped that maybe she could rekindle the hope and optimism and openness that had been growing in her before she'd met Laurent, but her dates hadn't been a success. She'd felt too wary, had struggled to connect with them. Now she clung to the hope that maybe it was just a case that she'd tried dating too quickly and that with time she would be more open to a relationship...but she feared that maybe she would never find it inside herself to trust a man again. 'How about you? Are you seeing someone?' she countered.

Laurent stood and jumped onto the landing steps, jealousy coiling in his stomach. For the past year he'd immersed himself in work, driven by the need to prove himself as a worthy CEO, but now as he turned to find Hannah's eyes sparking with anger he realised it was also to distract himself from the pain he'd caused her. He held out his hand and Hannah reluctantly took it. When she leaped, her hand tightened for a split second on his but the moment her foot touched the step she snatched it away.

They stood facing each other, the air between them dense with tension.

Hannah's jawline tightened. 'So, are you dating someone?'

'I'm too busy with work.'

'You worked crazy hours in London—it didn't stop you dating then.'

'It's different now.'

'In what way?'

She was testing him, pushing him for an answer and he wasn't sure what her question really was.

'Running a family business is complicated.'

Her nose wrinkled at that.

He pulled in a breath and admitted, 'After what happened between us, I don't feel like dating.'

'Yet?'

Would he ever want to date again? Right now, he couldn't see himself wanting to ask another woman out. But he couldn't admit that to her so instead he simply shrugged.

She looked at him with a puzzled expression. 'You're the one who ended it.'

When he'd ended their relationship, he'd used the excuse of needing to focus on his new life in France. And the fact that they wanted different things in life, namely that he wasn't interested in marriage. He'd kept from her the actual reasons why he would never marry, how his trust in others had been destroyed as a teenager, because to do so would have meant revealing his true self to her, a self he spent most of the time trying to avoid.

They shifted apart at the sound of footsteps behind them. Gabriel, the owner of La Belle Epoque, greeted them warmly and guided them to an outdoor table with views of a weir and an old mill.

Local teenagers were playing in the river, laughing and calling to one another in the evening sunshine.

After Gabriel had taken their order and poured them a glass of white wine each, Hannah smiled as one of the teenagers swung over the river, whooping loudly before landing with an enormous splash in the water, which earned her applause from her gang. 'When we were teenagers and the weather was fine, I used to go down to the river that ran through our land with Cora and Emily to swim and hang out. Did you and François do the same?'

'We spent our summers with my grandparents in Paris.'

She placed her elbow on the table and balanced her chin in the cup of her hand. 'I thought Parisians left the city for the summer. Why didn't they come here?'

'My grandparents moved to Paris after my father took over the family business.' He stopped with the intention of saying no more, but thanks to Hannah's expectant silence he found himself eventually admitting, 'There were arguments. My grandfather didn't approve of how my father was running the business, so they moved away. When we were old enough I asked my grandfather if François and I could spend the summers with them in Paris.'

'Did your parents not mind?'

He couldn't help but give a rueful laugh. 'They were too busy to even notice we weren't around.'

She grimaced but then, ever the optimist, asked with excitement, 'Did you like Paris?'

'We both loved it. François even stayed and finished his final years of school there.'

Her brows shot up. 'Wow, I couldn't see my parents agreeing to that—they even struggled when we left for university. Your parents obviously encouraged you to be independent.'

She was reading the situation all wrong. Not surprising given her background. Once again this evening he felt torn between changing the subject and telling her about his family. Before, he'd never felt that compulsion. In London, he'd been able to block out his past, but being back in Cognac for the past year had stirred up all the memories and emotions of how betrayed he'd felt by his parents' affairs.

'Is everything okay? You seem upset.'

He started at Hannah's words. She'd always been so good at reading his moods.

'Our family life was rather chaotic. I persuaded François he would do better in a calmer environment.'

'Have you always been the protective older brother?'

He grinned at the playfulness of her question. 'Probably.'

Hannah grinned back and then in a flash memories and attraction danced between them.

His throat tightened.

Hannah twisted her wine glass around and around. 'It was a shame you couldn't make Lara and François's civil ceremony in London last week. I know François was disappointed but at least your father was well enough to travel with your mother.'

'I was travelling in Asia—promoting the House.'

She snorted, clearly not buying his answer. 'I reckon, given your views on marriage, that you were simply avoiding the ceremony.'

'That's possibly true too.' Seeing her smile of satisfaction that she'd called it right, he added, 'But before you accuse me of disloyalty or not playing my part, can I point out that there is no tradition here in France of there being a best man at weddings? But as Lara is keen to have her sister as her bridesmaid, to keep some British traditions, I have agreed to be the best man.'

She laughed at that. 'You make it sound as though you have agreed to take a place on a battlefield.'

Was marriage, commitment, trusting in others, so easy for her? 'Did you mind being asked to be the wedding celebrant?'

'I was honoured. What else did you expect?'

He wanted to say that he thought she should

have said no to François and Lara. But instead
he said, 'Are you actually enjoying the work? It
can't be easy combining it with your day job.'

'You still don't understand why I want to be
a celebrant, do you?'

'It's not the career direction a young and successful finance director usually takes.'

Their conversation was interrupted by one of
the waiting staff arriving with their orders: *sal-
ade au saumon et l'avocat* for Hannah, double
carpaccio de boeuf for himself.

After they had eaten for a few minutes in silence, Hannah placed her cutlery on her plate
and said, 'I love being a wedding celebrant because I want to contribute something meaningful to people's lives.' She paused and looked at
him with a determined pride. 'I need something
positive and uplifting in my life.'

He lowered his own cutlery. 'I'm sorry that
I hurt you.'

She sat back in her chair, folded her arms and
stared towards the teenagers who were walking
home through the meadow on the other side of
the river. 'It's in the past.'

'We'll see each other in the future. I don't
want to cause you any further hurt.' For reasons he didn't understand he felt compelled to
add, 'Nothing has changed…there can be no
future for us.'

Her gaze flew back to him. Anger now sparked in her eyes. She stood. 'It's been a year. I'm over it… I'm over you, Laurent. I've moved on. Don't overinflate your importance in my life.'

CHAPTER THREE

THE FOLLOWING DAY, leaving his Sales and Marketing director to wrap up a meeting with the buyers from an international airline in the tasting room, Laurent rushed back to his office located in the recently opened modern extension he'd commissioned last year. Designed by world-renowned architect, Max Lovato, the acclaimed building was his signal to the world that Bonneval Cognac was about to retake its positon as the most exclusive cognac brand in the marketplace.

A wide walkway joined the second floor of the old cognac warehouse to the executive floor of the new building. Max's vision of the walkway resembling a floating garden had been realised thanks to an extensive and lush planting scheme of mature trees and plants that had produced an eye-watering bill.

Laurent rolled his shoulders against the financial pressures that perched there permanently these days like an overloud and insistent chatterbox parrot. Only time would tell if his ambitious and costly expansion and marketing strategy would pay off. If they didn't make the projected sales figures he'd forecast for this year, things could get very difficult. He would even have to seriously consider selling a share of the business. Which in his eyes would be nothing less than abject failure.

His assistant, Mila, rose from her chair when he entered her outer office and gave him an apologetic smile. He shook his head as if to say that he understood why she'd called him out of his meeting—they both knew of old how obstinate his father was.

When he entered his office he gritted his teeth at the sight that welcomed him—his father sitting behind his desk flicking through his paperwork. When was he going to accept his retirement, that Laurent and not he was now the CEO of Bonneval Cognac?

'Ah, Laurent.' His father gave him a smile, the left side of his mouth not rising quite as high as the right. Laurent felt his frustration ease at this reminder of his father's stroke, but it flourished again when his father added, 'You took your time.'

Laurent breathed down his irritation. 'I was meeting with AML Airlines. We're trying to persuade them to carry our XO Exclusif in their first-class cabins.' Seeing his father's sceptical expression, he added, 'Unfortunately we have a lot of ground to make up for the way their contract was managed in the past.'

'It was not our fault that our competitors undercut us.'

He bit back the temptation to laugh bitterly at his father's poor defence and said instead, 'We didn't negotiate the contract renewal properly. We backed them into a corner where they had no choice but to go with the competition.' He paused, about to say that living off past glories and perceived status had no place in today's business world.

For long seconds he and his father glared at one another. But then a discreet cough from behind him had him spin around to find Hannah.

He nodded in acknowledgement of her presence and received a lukewarm smile in response. She was still angry with him for reiterating last night that they had no future together. But he'd needed to say it, for his sake as much as hers— there was too much lingering physical attraction between them, which, thrown into the mix of the crazy emotions that came with a wedding and their forced proximity over the weekend, could lead them to doing something that they both regretted. After their dinner last night they had travelled back to the château in silence and he'd left for work this morning before dawn, leaving a note to say that he'd taken Bleu to stay with his friend Phillippe for the duration of her visit.

'This morning I gave Hannah a tour of the House.' Laurent turned his attention to his father, who added, 'Hannah was all alone in the château when your mother and I returned from Bordeaux. François and Lara were delayed in the city.' His father shook his head in reprimand. 'We can't have our house guests not entertained, Laurent. It's your duty as a host to ensure they're well cared for. I had planned on taking Hannah to lunch now but your mother is insistent that I return to the château—she's getting much too stressed about this wedding. I want you to take Hannah to lunch instead.'

Laurent was about to say no. He'd a string of meetings this afternoon he'd yet to prepare for. But he could tell his father was waiting for him to object. His father relished arguing with him. And he certainly wasn't going to embarrass Hannah by having an argument over who would take her to lunch.

Before he could say anything, though, Hannah stood. 'Antoine, I'll drive you home.' She gestured to his paper-strewn desk. 'I'm sure Laurent is busy.' Giving him a brief smile, she turned towards the door.

His father walked after her. 'I don't need you to drive me. I called François and told him to collect me on his way back from Bordeaux. He and Lara are downstairs waiting for me. You should see more of the town. You can accompany me downstairs on the way. I need to rush, though—apparently François and Lara are late for a meeting with their wedding planner.'

Hannah looked at him helplessly. Obviously waiting for him to argue against taking her. His father, meanwhile, looked all set to have an argument with him. 'It'd be my pleasure to take you to lunch.'

Hannah regarded him curiously. 'You never liked to take lunch in London.'

She was right. In London he'd worked at a furious pace; he still did so here, but he somehow also managed to fit in lunch and regular runs. He regarded Hannah, only now realising how well his new life suited him despite the pressures of his role. Aware of his father's keen gaze on them both, Laurent shrugged. 'I guess Cognac and the way of life here has changed me.'

For a moment he thought Hannah was going to ask what he meant but instead she held out her arm for his father to take.

Laurent grimaced and waited for his father to bat Hannah's arm away, as he did any other offer of help—he'd even thrown the walking stick his physio had given him out of one of the château's windows one day, and had grumbled like crazy when Bleu had gone and fetched it back.

But instead of rejecting Hannah's offer of assistance, his father placed his hand on her arm and Laurent followed them as they moved in the direction of the elevator, his father's limp slowing their progress.

Downstairs, his father chuckled when they walked outside to find François and Lara propped against the fountain in the entrance courtyard, arms wrapped around one another, Lara giggling as François whispered into her ear.

'*Le jeune amour est si puissant*...young love is so powerful,' his father said quietly.

Laurent rolled his eyes. His father certainly knew about love, or, in his case, lust and ego. Had he ever loved all those other women? In his teenage years, Laurent had been certain that his parents didn't love one another. How could they when they'd had those affairs? Yet they'd kept coming back to one another. And now, since his father's stroke, they were closer than ever. His head ached from trying to understand them. *Young love*—his gaze shifted to Hannah. She was the only woman he'd ever come close to loving.

His jaw tightened to see how she was watching Lara and François's playful flirting.

With a shriek, Lara broke away from François and ran to Hannah. The two women embraced, laughing and chatting over one another. Laurent looked away from the delight shining in Hannah's eyes, at the relief lightening her whole expression. It was as though in Lara she'd found a safe and secure harbour. Had she ever reacted like that with him? On occasion, but now, with the distance of time, he could see that even in the depths of their relationship Hannah had held herself back, as though uncertain of him. Why was that? Had she rightly sensed in him a man damaged by his past, a man who would bring her no happiness?

The Bonneval Cognac House was located on the outskirts of the town, its high greystone perimeter wall surrounded by pretty tree-lined roads and the Charente River to the south. When Hannah had driven the ten miles from the château to the House with Laurent's father, Antoine, this morning, for the first time since arriving in France she'd managed to relax, thanks to Antoine's easy company.

He'd surprised her by his quietness. When he and Laurent's mother, Mélissa, had arrived at the château he'd been like a whirlwind of charm and activity. But in the car after five minutes of idle chatter, he'd closed his eyes. She'd assumed he'd fallen asleep but as she'd slowed for a red traffic light as they'd neared the town, he'd said with his eyes still closed, 'I'm sorry for being such poor company. I get so tired at times.'

Hannah had been tempted to reach out and touch him, to respond to the bewilderment in his voice.

'It's okay. I enjoy silence, having time to think,' she'd said instead.

It was a while before he'd responded, 'You're sad.'

Hannah hadn't known how to answer, feeling completely undone by the simplicity of his statement. 'I was before.'

He'd opened his eyes at that, the intensity of the Bonneval blue-eyed gaze faded with him, but still more than capable of seeing through her pretence.

His quiet calm in the car, his attentiveness as he'd guided her around the distillery and the visitor centre had been so in contrast to his combative encounter with Laurent just now that she'd been thrown by the unexpectedness of it all.

Now as she watched Laurent open the rear door of François's car and his father's refusal to accept his offer of assistance to sit into the low seat, she wondered at their relationship.

Then, having waved the others off, Laurent asked her to wait a moment before he disappeared down a cobbled laneway at the side of the reception area.

A few minutes later he was back, now riding a sleek black Italian scooter. He handed her a white helmet to wear and then pulled on a black one himself. 'I have a meeting at two. Travelling by bike will save us from having to look for parking and we'll also be able to bypass the summer tourist traffic.'

This was not how she'd planned for this weekend to work out. At worst she'd thought she'd have to observe Laurent from a distance; now she was about to ride on a scooter with him. She yanked on her helmet, trying not to stare as he pulled off his silver tie and bunched it into his trouser pocket, releasing the top buttons of his white shirt, before pulling on a pair of mirrored aviators. Did he seriously have to look so hot all of the time? Did this man have any down days? Maybe this could be a form of aversion therapy? By spending all this time with him and how it reminded her of her previous heartache, then maybe she would develop an aversion to him.

She swung her leg over the scooter seat, glad she'd opted to wear her navy Bermuda shorts instead of the new white and blue summer dress she'd bought for the weekend. For the past month as the wedding weekend had loomed ever closer she'd found herself constantly drawn to the boutiques near her work at lunchtime. She'd go out with the intention of picking up a sandwich from her local favourite deli, only to find herself in a changing room trying to convince herself that she was only there to buy new things because her existing wardrobe was dated. When in truth this weekend had been the real reason. Her trips to the beautician and hairdresser had also ostensibly been about looking professional for the wedding, but whenever she looked into the mirror, she'd wondered what Laurent would think.

She edged herself back in the seat. As far away from him as possible, with the intention of holding on to the side of the seat, but Laurent's sharp right turn as they exited out onto the street soon had her clinging to his waist.

From the low-rise modern outskirts of the town they soon entered the old town, Laurent buzzing down narrow cobbled streets, past imposing centuries-old sandstone houses, many with ornate carvings around their doorways, past outside diners sheltering beneath sun umbrellas. They passed tourists staring into the windows of the specialist Cognac and Bordeaux wine sellers and elegantly dressed locals walking with purpose towards lunch dates.

Laurent came to a stop at a *fromagerie*.

From outside she watched him purchase some items while talking animatedly with the young blonde woman who served him. She looked away when the young woman waved out to her, annoyed with herself for feeling jealous.

Afterwards they drove along a maze of deserted alleyways, the restaurants and shops giving way to old stone warehouses, ancient pulley systems hinting at their previous use.

They came to a stop on a grassy bank by the river. Under the shade of a lime tree, he spread out their lunch of cheese, crackers, quince and a bottle of sparkling water each. She smiled and sat a distance away from him, trying not to show how thrown she felt that he'd chosen a picnic for them to share.

Laurent broke off a piece of *reblochon*, placed it on a cracker and handed it to her. At first they ate in silence, the only sound the roll of the river and birdsong from the trees lining the riverbank.

'It's so pretty here.'

Laurent grinned. 'Given your love of picnics, I thought you'd appreciate it.'

She bit into the cheese, trying to focus on the creamy texture and the nutty taste and not how her heart was melting at his warm smile, at the fondness in his voice. For want of a distraction she tentatively prodded the parchment paper of the other cheeses.

Laurent chuckled. 'I promise I haven't bought anything offensive.'

'I'm still terrified to open my fridge door.'

'Even a year later?' he asked, turning, his knee touching her thigh. Despite herself she jerked away.

She caught the disquiet that flashed in his eyes and said, 'Some fears are deeply ingrained.'

He picked up another cracker, placed a thin slice of quince paste and then some creamy Brie on top. She shook her head when he offered it to her, feeling undone by the intimacy of this picnic, the act of him preparing and offering her food.

'Dogs, pungent cheeses and hair down the plughole, I already know you fear all those... anything else you'd like to confess to?'

Reaching for a cracker and loading it with some more of the *reblochon* even though she really wanted to taste the Brie, she admitted, 'After my flight here, you can add turbulence— we were thrown around for a good ten minutes.'

Laurent's expression grew concerned. 'Were you hurt?'

'Luckily I had my seat belt fastened.' She shrugged, trying not to make a big deal of it, but in truth when the plane had been tossed around the sky she'd longed with every fibre of her being for his calm reassurance. And, tragically, seeing him again brought home the sad truth that every night for the past year when she'd come home from work to her empty apartment, she'd longed for his company. It was him she'd wanted when she'd read, heard or seen something that had fired her imagination and had been bursting to share it with someone. But he hadn't wanted her. She had to remember that. She rolled her eyes, forcing a light-hearted tone to her voice. 'I was okay until the guy next to me panicked and grabbed my hand. His grip was incredible. I had to ask him to let go after a while. He'd already told me that he was a fireman from York on the way to see his sister in Bordeaux. You'd think after five years of service turbulence wouldn't worry him.'

Laurent leaned back and threw her a sceptical look. 'That sounds to me like a perfect excuse to flirt with you.'

She was still smarting from what he'd said last night at the restaurant about them not having a future. She hated his assumption that she might even think that that was a possibility, hated that he'd no understanding that there was no way she'd ever allow herself to fall in love with him again, hated that he must have been alarmed enough by her obviously poor attempt to disguise her attraction to him to even say it… Had she given him some unconscious sign? Had she stared at him too much in the boat, been too jumpy around him? So she said, 'He did ask for my number when we landed.'

He leaned towards her, his expression a mixture of incredulous and irritated. 'I hope you didn't give it to him.'

Deciding not to answer his question, just to rile him, she said instead, 'I loved my tour of the Cognac House earlier. Your father was a great host, fun and full of great stories.'

He picked up a cracker and snapped it in two. 'He's always had an eye for a pretty woman.'

Hannah couldn't help but laugh at his disgruntled tone. 'I think we both know that I was a convenient way for him to escape the château and your mother's long list of things she wanted him to do.'

Throwing his head back, Laurent took long annoyed gulps of his water. Confused by how agitated he was at her mention of his father, she felt a desire to try to understand their relationship. She knew from their time together that he didn't have an easy relationship with his parents, his father in particular, but he'd never gone into specifics; instead he'd shrugged and said that his parents were different from him.

When he'd learned of his father's stroke, however, he'd been visibly upset. He had called her in her office, told her what had happened, and that he needed to leave for France immediately. Hannah had gone to his house, wanting to comfort and support him, but he'd rushed about packing, shutting down any attempts she'd made to discuss how he was feeling. He'd barely hugged her before he'd run out to the awaiting taxi. After that day, things had changed between them. He'd grown distant from her. Constantly preoccupied, he'd flown home to Cognac at every possible opportunity.

'He said he's probably never going to be able to drive again.'

Laurent let out a sigh. 'It's what frustrates him most.'

'Losing that freedom must be hard.'

Arching his head back, he stared up at the canopy of the tree for a few moments before saying, 'He's certainly making life hard for those around him.'

After his father's stroke, she'd once suggested to Laurent that she travel with him to Cognac but he'd said it wasn't a good idea. She'd tried to hide how hurt she was, tried to remain supportive, but increasingly she'd known that he was excluding her from his life. Now, having seen his home here, the vastness of the Cognac House, his place as CEO of such a prestigious brand, she understood why he'd seen no place for her here. She cleared her throat, trying to focus on their conversation, and asked, 'In what way?'

Propping himself back on his elbows, Laurent stretched his legs out on the grass. 'For a start he doesn't accept that he's no longer CEO of the House.'

Distracted by the sight of his long legs, the narrowness of his hips and waist in his grey trousers, the gleam of light shining from the silver buckle of his belt, remembering all the times she'd clumsily, desperately, unbuckled his belts in the past, she asked weakly, 'Can he take on another role?'

'And give him a legitimate reason to come in and interfere? I don't think so.'

His shirt was pulled tight across his chest, revealing the outline of taut skin and defined muscle beneath. She shifted on the grass, and against her better judgement angled herself a fraction closer to him, a thrilling sensation flourishing in her limbs. 'All of his experience could be a valuable asset to the business.'

His gaze lingered on her silver ankle bracelet. His blue gaze was darker than usual when he looked back up. 'I don't remember you ever wearing an ankle bracelet before.'

There was a low and seductive timbre to his

voice. Her heart turned over. 'I spent the New Year in India. I bought it there as a memento.'

He sat up, leaning back on one arm. 'Did you go alone?'

'The yoga teacher I follow online, Kim Ackerman, was running a week-long course there, so I signed up for it.' She was tempted to add that it was the online videos from Kim, a London-based online yoga superstar, that had kept her sane for the past year—chasing away the memories of him that had threatened to subsume her, replacing her regrets with a more productive mindset of being grateful for what she had in life and the opportunities out there waiting for her to grab hold of. 'It was a spur-of-the-moment decision. I decided I couldn't take any more of the wet weather we were having.' She shifted away from him again, the chemistry between them making her way too jumpy. 'There must be a role in the company your father could take on with all of his experience.'

He ran a hand tiredly against his jawline and for a moment she thought he wasn't going to answer her, but then he said quietly, 'My father almost brought the business to ruin.'

'I didn't realise…'

He shook his head. 'You had no reason to.'

'Am I right in guessing that you have a strained relationship with him?'

He laughed at her question. 'That must be hard for you to comprehend, given how well you get on with your parents.'

Despite his laughter, his voice contained an edge, a disappointment, a hurt that stabbed at her heart. 'It's a shame you don't get along—is it the fact that you've taken over as CEO? In my work I often deal with family businesses. It's not unusual for there to be conflict between generations, especially when the younger one takes over. It's hard for the older generation to let go and for the younger people to listen to advice.'

He eyed her with exasperation. 'Trust me, it has nothing to do with me not listening. The issues between us go back decades.' A tic appeared on the ridge of his jawline. 'Both of my parents had affairs when I was a teenager and left each other. When the affairs petered out they would eventually return.'

Hannah startled at the raw hurt in his voice. 'Seriously?'

Laurent's eyes widened. She flinched at the crassness of her response.

'Would I joke about something like that?'

She shook her head, seeing the hurt in his eyes, her heart pulling, her mind racing to understand what it would do to a teenager to experience such turmoil. Emotion clumped in her throat—anger and sadness and compassion for a teenage Laurent trying to deal with his parents' affairs; upset and regret that he'd never felt able to tell her any of this before now. She leaned towards him, her fingers brushing against his thigh. His eyes met hers. Softly she whispered, 'That must have been so painful for you.'

Bewildered, Laurent felt the electric charge of Hannah's touch, trying to reconcile it with the empathy in her eyes. He never spoke about his past. Why then was he telling this woman whom he knew he needed to keep his distance from? His mind reeling, he knew he had to somehow downplay it all. 'It was chaotic. Escaping to Paris to stay with our grandparents helped to bring back some normality. That's why I encouraged François to stay there.'

'Why didn't you?'

'I came back to Cognac in the hope of persuading my father to hand over the business to me.' He began to fold up the cheeses in their parchment paper, placing them back into the paper bag, thrown by the realisation that it was more than just that. He'd returned because he'd feared for his mother, who had always become withdrawn and silent whenever his father left the family home. 'From the age of sixteen I worked in every operation in the business from the distillery to the warehouses and Admin. I wanted to know every facet of the business inside out. When I turned twenty my grandfather and I made one final attempt to persuade my father to hand the business over to me but he refused. I left for Paris after that and then London. Staying in Cognac was pointless. The only reason I'm CEO now is because of his stroke. It was a decision forced upon him.'

'That annoys you?'

He blinked at her question. He'd assumed his issues with his father were because of the past, but with Hannah's question he realised it was also about his father's lack of acknowledgement and recognition of everything he was doing to turn the business around. 'He doesn't trust me and questions every decision I make.'

He stood and went to a nearby bin, throwing the bag of half-eaten cheeses into it.

Hannah was waiting at the scooter when he turned around. She handed him his helmet and asked gently, 'Are you enjoying the role of CEO?'

That was the first time anyone had asked him that question, the first time he'd stopped to consider it himself. 'Yes, I am. We're slowly turning the business around. I've appointed some new talent who are as keen as I am to see the business thrive. We've a great team with a world-class product.' He paused as a sense of ease, almost the freedom of self-determination, swept over him in acknowledging to himself the job satisfaction the role was giving him. Then his heart lurched at Hannah's smile at his words, at her obvious pleasure that he was enjoying the role. For some reason he wanted to include her in the conversation, to, in a small way, let her know that he still thought about her. 'I travel a lot with the role. I try to incorporate some downtime in the places I visit, especially to go and see any alternative museums.'

A glint sparked in her eye. 'I bet none have been as exciting as the lawnmower museum we visited in Finland.'

He grinned. 'Well, I did visit a museum of bad art in Berlin and a balloon museum in Perth.'

She gave him a teasing smile. 'And to think how you used to complain when I dragged you to museums in the past.'

'What can I say? You converted me to the more quirky places.' He was tempted to tell her that when he'd visited the museums he had missed her laughter, the serious way she would read out the exhibition notes, loving the peculiar facts.

'I'm jealous. They sound really cool.' Her hand coming to rest on the gear shift of the scooter, she gave him a tentative smile. 'Why did you never tell me about your childhood when we were together?'

'There was never any real cause to.' Which

was the truth. But not the full story. How could he tell a woman who had grown up in a text-book happy family the truth of his dysfunctional one? What would have been the point?

'But you have now,' she said.

'In London, I didn't handle our split well. I was distracted by my father's illness, taking over as CEO, wrapping up my affairs in London. I should have explained myself better. I saw how unhappy and chaotic my parents' lives were, growing up. I don't want any of that… I can't give you what you want in life—marriage, commitment.'

'Trust me, Laurent, I'm more than aware of that fact. Anyway, I don't recall ever asking you for those things.' With an angry tilt of her chin, she asked, 'So, are you enjoying being back in Cognac? Do you miss London at all?'

Mixed with the irritation of her question was a hint of wistful hope. Softly, not wanting to hurt her, he answered the truth. 'I feel completely at home here. I hadn't realised just how much I missed Cognac when I was away. It's where I belong. Bonneval Cognac is my legacy. I passionately want to make it a success.' He rubbed a hand at the tension in his neck rather than give into the temptation of reaching over and touching the soft skin of her cheek in a bid to wipe away the frustration in her expression.

'There are aspects of London that I miss greatly, but the decisions I took when coming back to Cognac were the right ones.'

She worked her jaw, unhappy with his answer. 'You say Bonneval Cognac is your legacy but who will inherit the business if you don't believe in love, in marriage? Or will you have children regardless of all that?'

'Look, up until my father became ill, it was never certain I would inherit the business in the first place. I think for now I should concentrate on having a business to pass on. Who actually inherits it is a far-off issue that doesn't concern me right now.'

She stepped back from the scooter. 'François is so eager and happy to marry… How can two brothers be so different in their views on relationships?'

He grimaced at her question. 'When something is wrong in your life, it can make you reject it even more fiercely or the exact opposite— crave it with all your being.' She frowned in confusion so he added, 'Our teenage years were extremely volatile. My guess is that François is looking for security.'

She shook her head and laughed. 'I'm sure François has more reasons to marry than just looking for security.' She paused before adding, 'You really are cynical about love, aren't you?'

He raised a sceptical eyebrow. 'What other reasons would he have to marry?'

She blinked at his question. 'Shared dreams, friendship, companionship, loyalty, commitment… love. Will that do, or do you want me to list even more?'

'And what happens when it all goes wrong?'

'It doesn't have to.'

'More than a third of marriages here in France end in divorce.'

Hannah stared at him, the anger in her expression shifting to frustration and then sad resignation. Pulling on her helmet, she said, 'I need to get back to the Château to prepare for the wedding rehearsal later this evening.'

In no mood to prolong this conversation he jumped onto the bike and fired the engine. They were driving back towards the old town centre, her warm palms disturbingly placed on his waist, when he heard her say, 'Maybe someday you'll meet the right person who'll change your mind.'

CHAPTER FOUR

OUT BEYOND THE dining room, the softly lit swimming pool beckoned Hannah. She shifted in her seat, the silk skirt of her halter-neck dress welding to her legs. What she wouldn't give to stand and run across the lawn, unzipping her dress and tossing it aside, before diving into the water. The cool water would wash away the unbearable heat of the night. Wash away her exhaustion from trying to converse in French. The seating plan for the rehearsal dinner taking place in the formal dining room of the château had placed her at the centre of the long dining table, Nicolas Couilloud, a business associate of the Bonneval family, on her right, a school friend of François's from Paris on her left. Both men had spoken of sport and politics all night and Hannah had struggled to keep up, with her schoolgirl French.

The blissful pool water might also wash away her ever-growing anxiety about tomorrow. The earlier rehearsal hadn't gone to plan. To start with they hadn't been able to locate Antoine and Lara's dad. When the errant fathers had eventually returned to the château Lara's dad had sheepishly admitted that they had gone to visit a friend of Antoine's who owned a nearby vineyard and had stopped to taste some of his cellar. Lara and François had been decidedly tetchy and the whole rehearsal had been conducted with a frostiness in the air. Hannah had tried to lighten the mood but no one else had been inclined to follow her lead. And Laurent's silent and brooding presence hadn't helped matters either. Having him standing beside François and continually stare at her had caused her to stumble over her words.

What if the same happened tomorrow? What if she failed to capture the magic of the event? The wedding celebrant was like the conductor of an orchestra; it was she who would set the tone of the wedding. What if she messed up? Messed up in front of her best friend and the two hundred and fifty influential guests. Messed up in front of Laurent.

She cast her eye around the rest of the table. No one else seemed inclined to leave even though the meal had ended over an hour ago. Would they notice if she slipped away to work on her blessing speech? She still wasn't certain it fully captured the essence of Lara and François's relationship.

The seating plan had placed the younger generation to her left—the tension of earlier forgotten, Lara and François were chatting with their close friends who had travelled from around the world to celebrate with them. And to her right were Lara's and François's parents along with old family friends and associates, all busily chatting.

It was only she and Laurent who seemed like lone islands cast aside from the noisy anticipation that came before a big life event. Laurent was seated at the head of the table. At the pre-dinner drinks on the terrace he'd easily moved between the guests, being his usual charming self. It was only when Nicolas Couilloud had taken him aside and spoken to him that Hannah had seen him tense. He and Nicolas had ended their conversation with much shaking of heads. Instinctively she'd moved towards Laurent wanting to ask if everything was okay but, on seeing her approach, he'd turned away and spoken instead to Lara's sister and bridesmaid, Stella.

Already halfway across the terrace, suddenly without purpose, Hannah had faltered before she'd forced herself to continue, skirting past Laurent and Stella without a glance in their direction, hoping it looked to the other guests as if it had been her intention to step inside the château all along. She'd washed her trembling hands in the downstairs cloakroom, trying not to think about how beautiful twenty-four-year-old Stella looked in her red silk sheath dress with its daring slash to the thigh.

She had to give Laurent his due. He was doing an excellent job at avoiding her this evening. Which she should welcome. Wasn't that what she wanted after all—for them to keep their distance from one another? But it was so at odds with the intimacy of their conversation at lunchtime. Was he regretting having been so open with her?

She closed her eyes for a moment. Suddenly exhausted by this whole weekend. Exhausted by the wealth and culture of Laurent's life now. The opulence of the dining room, the sophistication oozing from the other guests, all reminders of the contrasting squalor of her early years. This wasn't her world. Even after she'd been rescued she'd been brought up in the warm simplicity of country life. Her dad wouldn't know a derivative, a Chagall, the difference between a Saint-émilion and a Médoc, even if they all bit him on the bottom. And she loved him for that. Love, loyalty, family and his animals were all that mattered to him.

She was also exhausted from being so physically close to Laurent. Not only was she struggling to contain her attraction to him, but after what he'd told her today, opening himself up to her, she stupidly, crazily, felt more connected to him. The very opposite of what she'd hoped to achieve this weekend.

Why was this weekend turning out so different from how she'd imagined it would? Only this evening, Lara had decided, with the encouragement of her parents and in a nod to tradition, that she should spend tonight away from François. So now Lara, Stella and their parents were spending the night with Laurent's parents in their lodge but there weren't enough beds for Hannah to move too. It shouldn't matter but she felt excluded by this change of plans. The vulnerability, that deep fear of disconnection that sat at the core of her being, was being stirred back into life by this weekend and she hated how out of control it made her feel.

She opened her eyes. Blinked at the brightness of the room and then was dazzled by the opulent diamonds hanging from the ears and throat of Nicolas Couilloud's wife sitting opposite her.

Her gaze unconsciously moved up the table, past the other guests, her heart performing an impressive leap to find Laurent staring towards her with concern. She twisted away, trying to tune back into the conversation between Nicolas and a glamorous French movie star seated across the table from him about redevelopment plans in Cannes, where they both owned summer houses, which they were vehemently opposed to, grumbling about the effect on the already chaotic traffic.

Laurent stood. Immediately all of the chatter around the table died as all heads turned in his direction. Was it his height, his powerful build, his ridiculously masculine features that were so exaggerated and beautiful that when people first met him they were often silenced by the need to study him, or was it simply his aura of command that so effortlessly had people respond to his movement?

He gave them a smile. A closed-mouth smile. The smile he gave when being polite. 'Thank you for coming to dinner tonight. I hope you've had an enjoyable evening.' He paused and nodded in the direction of François and Lara, his smile widening in affection. 'But as we have an important and busy day ahead of us tomorrow we need to draw this night to a close.'

The guests nodded, chairs moved backwards, some of the women picked up their evening purses, but all came to a stop when from the opposite end of the table Antoine called out, 'One more drink out on the terrace.'

For the briefest moment a pulse twitched at the side of Laurent's jawline. 'We can party tomorrow. For now, we all need to rest.'

Antoine stood. The entire table swivelled in his direction. 'One more won't do us any harm.'

Now everyone turned back towards Laurent and waited for his response. His eyes narrowed.

Without thinking Hannah stood. 'As wedding celebrant I agree with Laurent. I don't want any of you tired tomorrow.' She smiled at a frowning Antoine. 'I'm expecting you to dance with me, Antoine.'

Antoine's blue eyes twinkled. 'It will be my pleasure.'

Hannah said her goodbyes to her dinner companions and then, after a quick hug with Lara, encouraging her to try and get some sleep, she slipped out of the dining room before everyone else, averting her gaze when she saw Laurent unhappily follow her hasty departure.

Laurent went to knock on Hannah's bedroom door but at the last second pulled his hand away. In the aftermath of their lunch, as the hours had passed by in a blur of work meetings and telephone calls, a chasm had opened up in him as to the wisdom of having been so frank with Hannah. Would she think less of him, knowing his background? Now, after deliberately keeping his distance from her all evening, was he really about to throw all of that good work away? It was an easy question to answer. The tension that had been etched on her face earlier when she'd sat with her eyes closed at the dining table was too profound to ignore.

He knocked on the door. Swallowed when the consideration that Hannah might answer the door in her nightwear dawned on him. Despite himself he smiled at that thought.

The door swung open. Hannah eyed him, her gaze narrowing when it honed in on his smile. She folded her arms. He mirrored the action, propping himself against the doorframe, unbalanced not for the first time at how striking she looked in her figure-hugging knee-length purple halterneck dress that accentuated every glorious curve of her body. The urge to step forward and release her hair from its tight bun had him tense every muscle in his body. 'I had the situation downstairs under control.'

She raised an eyebrow. 'Have you come all the way to my room to tell me that?'

Despite himself he laughed at her deadpan expression. Then, taking in the paperwork in her hand, he said, 'Come outside, there's something I want to show you.'

She shook her head. 'I need to prepare for tomorrow's ceremony.'

'You're nervous about tomorrow.'

She stepped back. 'No, I'm not.'

He pushed away from the doorframe. 'Come outside—what I have to show you might help you relax.'

Shoving a hand onto her hip, she answered, 'For the last time, I don't need to relax.'

Something about the tilt of her hip got to him. Shrugging off his tuxedo jacket, he stepped into the room and threw it onto the back of a bedroom chair. His bow tie soon followed.

She looked at the jacket and his bow tie with dismay. 'What the hell are you doing?'

Her horrified expression only fuelled his need to push her to be honest. 'This damn heat. Prove to me that you're okay about tomorrow by coming with me.'

She gave him a disbelieving look before slamming her paperwork down on the bedroom console table next to her open laptop and then storming out of the door. He walked behind, his eyes taking in the angry sway of her hips as she hurried along the corridor and down the stairs in her high heels.

The château was silent. Earlier, François and he had waved all the guests goodbye, but no sooner had the tailgate lights of Lara's parents' car disappeared in the direction of his parents' lodge when François had raced to his car, shouting that he needed to see Lara one more time.

Laurent had stood watching the trail of François's tail lights, envying his brother's ability to throw himself into love so wholeheartedly. But then he'd shivered despite the heat of the night and prayed that life would be good to François and Lara, that time, and the dimming of passion, the reality of committing yourself to another person for eternity, the lure of others, the selfishness that was at the core of every human being, would not destroy their marriage.

Outside he led Hannah in the direction of the estate's farm. The farm's single and double stone outbuildings were built around a cobbled courtyard, a water pump in the centre. Opening the door of one of the smaller buildings, he stepped inside, to a chorus of chirping, inhaling the scent of the heavy blanket of fresh straw on the floor.

She paused at the entrance and gave him a dubious look. Then as she peered through the doorway her expression lit up. 'Oh, wow, they're so beautiful,' she whispered, taking small tentative steps towards the hen and her seven yellow fluffy chicks.

Stopping a distance away from them, she crouched down and watched the chicks stumble around their mother, chirp, chirp, chirping away. 'When did they hatch?'

The knuckled wave of Hannah's spine was exposed by a gap in the back of her dress. He swallowed against the memories of running his fingers along her back when she lay beside him, a slow sexy smile forming on her lips when it was a prelude to sex, a sated smile when it was in the aftermath. He stuffed his hands in his pockets and walked to stand next to her. 'Earlier today.'

She stood. 'They're adorable, but why did you bring me to see them?'

'Remember the endless photos of newborn animals that your mum sent to you, which you then forwarded on to me? I thought seeing these little guys might help you forget about tomorrow.'

She eyed him curiously. 'Do you think I *should* be nervous?'

'You'll ace tomorrow.' He paused and watched the chicks stumble away from their mother and then with a jolt of alarm race back to her as though terrified they were about to lose her. Then turning to Hannah, the unease in her brown eyes slamming into his heart, he added, 'You're amazing. Always remember that.'

Reddening, Hannah gave a faint smile and backed towards the door. Outside she looked around the near-empty courtyard, a single tractor the only sign of any farming activity. 'I'm guessing there isn't a working farm here any more?'

'There was in my grandfather's time. My father let it go. I've recently employed a farm manager. He's reintroducing some livestock. I want the château to be self-sufficient.'

She nodded to this. 'Good idea.' The night sky was clear, a fat moon shedding bright light down on their surroundings. Into the quiet of the night she said in an almost whisper, as though she was telling him something very intimate, 'The option of moving to Singapore isn't the only one I'm considering. I'm also thinking about moving to Granada in Spain to become a full-time wedding consultant.'

'Really? Your career is in the city. Why would you give up everything you've achieved?'

She shrugged, the long delicate lines of her exposed collarbone lifting and falling. 'I fell in love with Granada when I was there for Emily's wedding. It would be an exciting option, a new start for me.'

He'd always thought of her as being ambitious in the corporate world only. These new ambitions made him uneasy. Unfairly and irrationally, he hated the idea that she was forging a new and unexpected life. 'What about your promotion? Your transfer to Singapore?'

'Granada is only a short flight away and Emily and her husband are planning on buying a holiday home there. Singapore is so far away from everyone I love.' Wounded eyes met his for a moment. Guilt and regret slammed into his chest. Then with a brief grimace she added, 'Do you want to talk about your conversation with Nicolas Couilloud earlier?'

When they had dated, they had been a sounding board for one another over work issues. Hannah's advice had always been solid. For a moment he considered telling her, realising how much he missed having someone to talk to about issues that were troubling him. But talking about work would feel as though they were dropping back into their old relationship. 'It's just a business issue.'

'A sizeable business issue, I'm guessing.'

He gestured for them to walk back through the lightly wooded copse that separated the farm buildings from the château. He tried to resist talking but Hannah's patient silence, the worry, the frustration of his discussion with Nicolas had him eventually blurt out, 'Nicolas is one of my father's oldest friends but he also owns the company who distributes our cognacs. He's vital in our supply chain. He has the whole market sewn up—he has no competitors with the same market reach. He told me tonight that he's going to increase his fees when our contract with him is up for renewal next month.'

They emerged from the shade of the copse. Hannah came to a stop and asked, 'Why?'

'He's citing increased transportation costs.'

'You don't believe him?'

He inhaled a deep breath, frustration clogging his lungs. 'I can't help but think that it has something to do with my father.'

Hannah's eyes widened. 'Surely not. Why would Antoine have anything to do with Nicolas's decision?'

He could not help but smile at Hannah's innocence, part of him deeply envying her for never having experienced the soul-destroying destructiveness of a dysfunctional family.

'Why are you smiling?'

He jolted at the anger in Hannah's voice. Then, shrugging, he walked away, answering, 'Not all families are sweetness and light.'

She caught up with him on the terrace. 'Do you think that I'm that naïve, that I don't understand how people hurt others driven by their ego, by fear, by insecurity? I've seen it time and time again in my work, partnerships falling apart, family businesses not surviving. And do you know what the common denominator in all of it is? A lack of communication, a lack of connection and honesty.'

He sat on the arm of an outdoor sofa and crossed his arms. 'Being an outsider is easy. Try getting mangled up in the politics and personalities and history of a family business—then such logical analysis goes right out of the door. My family aren't like yours...so bloody normal.'

Hannah eyed him angrily before shifting her gaze towards the pool and the river beyond. She folded her arms, her delicate chin jutting out furiously. 'There's nothing normal about my family.' She paused and then added softly, 'My real family.'

Laurent stood. Confused by her words. 'Real family?'

She bit her lip, her gaze refusing to meet his. Silence descended between them. He waited, thrown by the emotion playing out in her expression as she made several attempts to answer his question. Eventually she answered in a faint whisper, 'I'm adopted.'

His brain tried to process what she'd said. 'Adopted?'

Her gaze met his, a flicker of disappointment soon being replaced by anger. 'Yes. Adopted. It happens.'

'You never said before...why not? *Dieu!* Why not?' He knew he was saying the wrong things but frustration, the awful feeling he hadn't known Hannah at all, drove him on, 'Why tell me now?'

She blinked at his questions. 'After what you told me today about your parents... I guess it seemed right that you know.'

He cringed at the now calm softness of her voice, which only emphasised his own angry torrent of questions. He breathed in and out to the count of four, trying to focus on Hannah rather than his hurt that she'd never told him before. He sat on the sofa properly, gestured that she should sit on a chair opposite.

Reluctantly she did so.

'What age were you?'

She raised a hand and kneaded her collar-bone. 'Seven.'

For a moment he flailed for the right way to talk about it all. He'd been an insensitive sod up until now and he desperately wanted to get this right. He gritted his teeth against the ball of failure that was rapidly growing in his gut— what type of boyfriend had he been that Hannah had never felt inclined or able to tell him this before? 'What happened?'

For a moment her concentration seemed to be on running her fingertips against the interwoven rattan reeds of her chair. But then she tilted her head in his direction, pride burning from her eyes. 'My birth parents were both drug users.

My memories are hazy, as you can imagine, but I remember a lot of parties and being left alone in the house on many occasions.' She stopped and swallowed. Her bottom lip gave a quiver. 'One night the police came and took me away.'

'You were scared.'

She gave a humourless laugh. 'Terrified.'

He fell back into his chair and stared up at the night sky for a brief moment. Then with a sigh he sat forward. 'I'm so sorry, Hannah. I wish you had told me before now.'

'What difference would it have made?'

Her question was a challenge. She wasn't hiding that fact in her direct gaze as she waited for his response, in the tension of her body, one leg wrapping around the other tightly at the calf. Would knowing about her adoption have changed anything? He swallowed and admitted, 'Maybe I would have been kinder...maybe I would have taken better care not to hurt you.'

Hannah's heart crumbled at the softness of Laurent's tone, at the sincerity of his expression. But at the same time her brain stirred in indignation and demanded that she show some pride. 'For crying out loud, Laurent, I don't need your pity just because I was adopted.' She sat forward in her seat, keen to change the subject, keen to bury the past once again, and the vulnerability and emptiness and confusion that arose in her any time she unearthed it all. 'If Nicolas ups the cost of distribution, what will be the impact on the business?'

Laurent eyed her with bewilderment. 'That's not of importance right now.'

She forged on. 'Will you speak to your father about it?'

He paused for a moment, clearly toying with whether to allow her to change the subject, but then with a sigh admitted, 'For all I know my father could be behind this price increase.'

Her mouth dropped open. Was he being serious? 'Why would he do that?'

His expression darkened at her disbelief. Tensely he answered, 'My father didn't want me to take over as CEO. It was my mother who insisted upon it. He would love to see me fail.'

Hannah shook her head. 'Are you sure? Maybe your father knows nothing about it. Why not at least talk to him? Maybe he has some advice he can pass on to you. Surely he doesn't want to see the business struggle…which I'm guessing it will, based on how anxious you looked all night.'

'I did?'

She could not help but smile at his annoyance that she'd spotted his tension. 'Don't worry, no one else would have noticed. But I know the signs—your right eye twitches.'

He crossed his arms. 'It does not.'

She laughed. 'Yes, it does.'

He shook his head but his bright blue eyes gave away his amusement. Then softly he said, 'We did have some fun times together, didn't we?'

Her smile faded. She swallowed at the fondness in his eyes. Despite herself she heard herself admit, 'Yes, we did.'

He gave her one of his wide-mouthed smiles that always reduced her to putty. 'Do you remember the night we went kayaking on Lake Saimaa?'

Hannah smiled in remembrance of the stunning beauty of the crystal-clear Finnish lake and exploring it under the summer midnight sun. 'How could I forget? It was magical.'

'And the time we went snowboarding in Ještěd?'

Hannah grimaced. 'I reckon the locals are still deaf from my screaming.' She paused and threw him an accusatory glare. 'And you were all Mr Cool, zipping around the place, showing off.' She could see that he was about to object, so she interjected, 'Never mind the travel, what I miss is having a gorgeous meal cooked for me in the evenings. You've ruined me to the pleasure of a ready meal for ever.' Only when she'd said those words did she cringe and wonder why she did.

She sighed in relief when he laughed and added, 'And I miss having you there in the mornings to pick out my ties.'

She shook her head. 'I'm still convinced that you're colour-blind.'

He stood and held out a hand to her, to help her rise. She took it, every cell in her body responding to its familiar strength. She went to take her hand away, but Laurent tightened his grip and stepped even closer. For long seconds he studied her, his blue gaze quickening her heart, sending fire into her belly. The scent of lavender hung heavily in the air, almost drugging in its density. In a low voice he eventually said, 'You never answered my question as to whether you're seeing anyone.'

Heat formed on her cheeks. Her throat grew dry. He always had this effect when he stood this close, when he spoke, when his eyes played games with her heart. She lowered her gaze to his mouth. She wanted to kiss him. She wanted to kiss him hard and remind him of everything he walked away from. But instead she whispered, 'Stella is young—don't break her heart.'

He let out a low disbelieving sigh and said in a grumble, 'She's at least ten years younger than me.'

'Eight actually, which is nothing.'

He inched forward, forcing her to tilt her head

to meet his stare. 'I'm not interested in Stella.' Heat and chemistry and emotion whirled and twisted around them.

Hannah blinked, trying to shake off the hot need burning through her veins, the cloud of desire that was fogging her brain to everything but the desire to feel his lips, to touch the hard muscle of his body. Just for one more time. What was the harm?

She leant forwards and then up onto her tippy-toes. His eyes darkened. She angled her head, shifted an inch away from his mouth. Her head swam with his nearness, with his familiar scent and heat. With a whimper of annoyance she placed her mouth on his.

It took a few seconds for her to realise that he wasn't responding to her kiss.

He didn't want this.

Shame exploding in her chest, she went to pull away.

But at her movement his arms wrapped around her waist, stopping her, and he kissed her with an urgency that had her instantly on fire. Her breasts, pushed hard against his chest, immediately felt tender and desire trickled through her body like an illicit pleasure. His kiss grew ever more hot and demanding and she met that demand, wanting to punish him. One hand wrapped around his neck, holding him closer, the other ran over the heat of his chest, past the soft leather of his belt and then lightly over his trousers, euphoria spreading through her when he groaned. She wanted to make love with him.

At that thought she broke away.

Panting hard, they stared at one another. What self-destructive part of her would sleep with him? Her ridiculous pride that wanted him to regret ending their relationship?

She flailed for something to say. Eventually she realised she could find a safe harbour in his business concerns. 'What's the worst-case scenario if Nicolas increases his fees?'

Laurent gave a disbelieving laugh. 'You kiss me and then ask a question like that.'

She decided to try to brazen this all out. 'To answer your earlier question, yes, I've been on dates, but none recently. I'm a young woman with desires.' She stopped as she inwardly cringed, before adding, 'I guess this wedding is bringing them out more than usual.'

Laurent's mouth dropped open. 'Are you propositioning me?'

'Are you kidding? It was a kiss. Nothing more. A moment of physical weakness from me. Don't get ahead of yourself.'

Laurent frowned. 'Hannah, you know—'

'Yes, yes.' Hannah interjected. 'Trust me, you

were more than clear about our future in London, just as clear last night and again today at lunchtime.' She winced at the bitterness in her voice and decided to change tack. 'Now, putting my professional hat on, can I advise that you speak to your dad? I know how difficult it is to put the past behind you, but surely the future is more important?'

With a look of exasperation he sighed. And then, his expression sobering, he considered her for much too long before asking gently, 'Are you in contact with your birth parents?'

Hannah eyed the main doorway into the château and the softly lit hallway beyond. She swallowed before she admitted, 'They both died. Soon after I was taken away my dad overdosed. My mum died ten years ago.'

'Dieu!'

Her gaze shot back to his, disappointment barrelling through her at the disgust in his voice. 'Not very pretty, is it?'

Laurent grimaced. 'I wish you had told me.'

Hannah edged towards the doorway, suddenly feeling beyond exhausted. 'Just as I wish you had told me about your childhood.' She gestured inside. 'I need to go and check over my paperwork for tomorrow.'

She'd stepped onto the marble floor of the

hallway when he called out, 'I thought we had known one another.'

She tried not to wince at the tired bewilderment in his voice. Turning, she nodded in agreement, her heart once again tumbling on seeing him. She forced herself to give him a smile of encouragement. 'Speak to your dad.'

He shook his head. 'I'll find a solution…by myself.'

Her exhaustion washed over her like a fresh wave. 'Do you let anyone into your life, Laurent?'

A deep frown bisected his forehead. 'Maybe it's safer not to let others in.'

She understood why he thought that way. She too carried hurt and pain and ghosts from the past. 'Perhaps it's safer, but I'm guessing it's an unhappier life for doing so.'

CHAPTER FIVE

THE FOLLOWING AFTERNOON, at the entrance to the walled garden, Laurent pulled François to a stop. François eyed him restlessly, keen to keep moving. Placing a hand on François's shoulder, Laurent looked him straight in the eye. 'Relax. Everything is going to be okay.'

François let out a frustrated breath. '*Dieu!* I feel sick with nerves.'

Laurent rolled his eyes, deliberately being obtuse. 'I still don't understand why you're insisting on marrying, but if you are going to do it at least try to relax and enjoy it.'

François shook his head and laughed. 'You're not fooling me, Laurent. I know how much you love Lara. Deep down I know you're happy to see us marry.'

Laurent held his hands up in defeat. 'Okay, I'll admit you two might actually make it work.'

François smiled triumphantly. 'I can't believe you've actually admitted that. You've made my day!' Then, looking down, he scuffed his shoe off the brickwork of the garden path before saying, 'It's good to have you by my side, you know.'

Laurent swallowed, taken aback by the affection in François's gaze. As brothers, they weren't given to displays of emotion. He lifted an eyebrow. 'I'm going to make you pay for it somehow.'

François laughed. 'I appreciate the supreme sacrifice you're making by being my best man.'

Laurent grinned at his brother but then, sobering, he said, 'Whatever my views on marriage, I do wish you and Lara every happiness.' Then taking a key from his tux jacket, he handed it to François. 'My wedding gift to you both: Villa Marchand. I've had it renovated for you.'

His eyes wide in surprise, François weighed the key in the palm of his hands and shook his head. It was a considerable time before he managed to say, in a voice choked with emotion, 'I'm lost for words... I've loved that house ever since I was a boy and Lara fell in love with it too when we visited there last summer.'

Laurent shrugged, trying to pretend not to be choked up at François's delight. 'I know. That's why I'm giving it to you. You can stay there tonight if you wish, rather than here in the château.' He gave François a grin. 'I thought you might like the privacy. Hannah visited the house with me Thursday night and suggested some items that Lara might enjoy, so the house is honeymoon ready.'

François grimaced. 'How are things between you two?'

'Awkward.'

'I saw you out on the terrace last night when I returned to the château.' François paused and threw him a questioning look. 'You seemed very close.'

Dieu! Did François see them kissing? 'What do you mean "close"?'

François stepped back from his growled question. 'You were chatting, oblivious to the fact that I'd walked out to say hello—what did you think I meant?'

Guilt and relief washed over Laurent. 'You should have interrupted us. It would have been nice to chat with you over a drink. And nothing is going to happen between myself and Hannah. Relax.'

'You were so good together—' François shook his head '—but I'm not going to lecture you again on all of that.' His expression hardening, François added, 'Don't hurt her.'

Memories of their kiss last night slammed into Laurent. Turning in the direction of the garden, he said, 'I have no intention of doing so.'

He walked away but when François did not follow he turned at the doorway to the garden to find his brother eyeing him sceptically. When François eventually decided to join him, he said, 'Lara needs Hannah in her life. Promise me that you won't make things any more awkward than they already are. Stay away from her, Laurent.'

Laurent tried to make an acquiescing noise. François raised an eyebrow.

With a sigh, Laurent relented and said, 'I promise.'

Seating had been arranged on the lawns either side of the central cobbled pathway. Bows had been tied onto the rose bushes dense with blowsy blooms that were planted at regular intervals along the herbaceous border, their heavy scent filling the air. At the wisteria-covered archway that led out to the lawns of the château, a pedestal and two gilt chairs had been placed for the blessing ceremony to take place.

Laurent's heart took a sizeable wallop when he spotted Hannah breaking away from a conversation with a friend of Lara's and walking towards the pedestal. Dressed in a knee-length pale pink dress, the fitted bodice emphasising her curves, the skirt flaring over her hips, her hair tied back into a sleek ponytail, she looked both professional and as sexy as hell.

Dieu! Their kiss last night had been unbelievable. Hot, sultry, beautiful. But it'd been too much of a reminder of how much he missed her. And not just physically. It had brought home how much he missed her warmth, her gentleness, her easy presence.

Moving towards the archway, François and he nodded hello to the already assembled and seated guests. But all the while, an invisible force was pulling him towards Hannah, who was checking through her paperwork.

Her gaze shifted upwards as their footsteps neared. She smiled warmly at François and, walking towards him, hugged him tightly. 'Gosh, you look incredibly handsome, François.'

Laurent blinked at the affection in Hannah's voice, at her calm enthusiasm.

François fiddled with the collar of his tux jacket, casting a critical eye down over his suit. 'Is everything looking okay?'

Hannah adjusted his bow tie a fraction. 'There, now you're perfect.'

Then, with an unenthusiastic glance in Laurent's direction, she returned to her paperwork.

He cursed under his breath. Today was going to be as awkward as he'd feared.

The arrival of his parents kept him busy for the next few minutes as he had to encourage his father along the path as he insisted on stopping and chatting to the guests, despite the fact that the ceremony was about to start at any minute. When he then tried to assist his father to sit, his father pushed his arm away, muttering that he wasn't an invalid.

Taking his seat beside François, he tried to tune into the chamber orchestra playing to the side, tried to find some reassuring words to say to François, whose legs were jigging like crazy. But time and time again his attention was drawn back to Hannah, who was going through a constant ritual of thumbing through her paperwork and then looking expectantly towards the entranceway before glancing back to her paperwork again.

Circulate. Mingle. Do his best man and host duties. And stay the hell away from Hannah. That was the plan of action for today he'd formulated in the middle of last night when unable to sleep, thanks to the after-effects of their kiss.

But it hadn't just been their kiss that had kept him awake. It was also the haunted look in Hannah's eyes when she'd spoken about her adoption. He'd caused her enough hurt as it was. He wasn't going to add to that tally by spending time with her, which would only be asking for trouble given the chemistry that whipped between them like a live coil.

His plan of action, which had made sense in the middle of last night, had one major flaw, however. It hadn't taken into account how alone and nervous Hannah would look as she stood waiting for Lara's arrival. He moved restlessly in his chair. Telling himself to stay put. The last thing they needed were wagging tongues from those who knew of their previous relationship.

Once again Hannah's gaze shifted down over the crowd, towards the entrance. A bumblebee flew close to her. She leapt backwards, flapping her hands wildly. The bee got the message and buzzed away. With a grimace Hannah glanced nervously out towards all the assembled guests before her hands gripped the wooden sides of the pedestal, her skin flushing.

Standing, he approached her, deliberately blocking her from everyone else's view. 'I know you are going to do an incredible job...' He paused, knowing he should step away now but Hannah's brown wide-eyed expression, and the way her dress gave a faint glimpse of the valley between her breasts, pierced through all his resolve to keep his distance. 'You're looking beautiful today.'

Hannah's hand shot from the side of the pedestal to switch off the microphone.

Dieu!

Hannah glared at him.

For a moment all he could hear was the orchestra's light playing. Maybe the guests didn't hear him. That brief glimmer of hope was soon dispelled, however, when sudden whoops and claps of approval thundered behind him.

He grimaced in apology. Hannah gave him one last glare before painting a calm professional smile on her face and looking beyond his shoulder as though waiting for a stage curtain to rise. He turned from her. Shrugged at the assembled guests, many of whom they had socialised with when they had visited François and Lara in Manchester and who had let it be known of their disappointment when their relationship had ended, trying to pretend that what he'd said wasn't of significance.

He retook his seat.

Leaning in towards him, François hit him with an exasperated stare. 'So much for promises.'

Hannah knew that it was a bride's prerogative to be late. But she wished with every fibre of her being that Lara would hurry up and arrive. She was already ten minutes late. Which under normal circumstances Hannah wouldn't even notice in the special hum and excited anticipation that came with the waiting for the bride.

Why did Laurent have to come up and speak to her? She'd just about been coping up until then. For a brief few seconds when he'd looked at her with that reassuring smile of his that had her heart turn over, his eyes soft and tender, she'd felt weak with relief that he was there to support her. But then he'd spoken and the dark edge in his voice when he'd said she looked beautiful had unsteadied her. And then the echo of his voice fading out over the sound system had registered. God, she couldn't bear the thought of people speculating incorrectly that their relationship might be back on. And now, there he was, sitting in front of her, looking all gorgeous and brooding in his tux, his black dress shoes shining brilliantly, his long legs spread out in front of him, his blue gaze continually glancing in her direction, making her already frayed nerves unravel even further.

She looked out over the guests and tried to maintain her professional smile. While inside she was a churning mess of emotions. Not only was she thrown by having Laurent so close by, but she still wasn't certain that her speech was any good. Was it just rambling thoughts? Would it have any meaningfulness for Lara and François?

Why did she feel so damn lonely, so vulnerable today? It felt as though a hole were opening up inside her. Would her relationship with Lara be the same once she was married? Had she been wrong in telling Laurent about her adoption? Had it really served any purpose? She'd wanted him to understand that she too knew of broken families. That it didn't have to define you. But she'd failed to explain all of that last night. Maybe her speech today might convey some of what she was trying to say.

Of course, the irony was that even though she believed your past didn't have to define your future, she knew only too well that putting that belief into practice was easier said than done. Some fears seemed to tether you to the past by their force.

Laurent turned in his chair and, looking towards the entrance, said something to François. Hannah smiled at François's nervousness. Laurent shifted around in his seat and for a moment their eyes met. Unaccountably, tears threatened at the backs of Hannah's eyes at the light smile he gave her. The loneliness inside her deepened.

She looked away. She was *not* going to think about how she used to sit in work meetings daydreaming of one day walking towards him, becoming his wife. She used to fantasise about her dress, what her bridesmaids would wear, marrying on her parents' farm and, God help her, making love to her new husband.

Now she pulled back from the impulse to roll her eyes at her own naivety.

A movement at the entranceway had her pause

and then she was smiling crazily, tears once again forming in her eyes as first Stella, dressed in a primrose-yellow midi-dress, walked down the path, soon followed by a beaming Lara on her father's arm. Her lace, full-skirted midi-dress was perfect for a summer wedding, as were the rosebuds threaded lightly through her blonde hair tied up in a loose chignon.

When Lara reached François, Hannah's heart swelled to bursting point at the love that shone in both of their eyes, at how they smiled at one another shyly. How glorious to know that you were going to spend the rest of your life with the person you so deeply loved.

Hannah gestured to them to take their seats before her. She returned Lara's excited smile. Hannah gave her ear a quick tug. Lara giggled. Ear tugging used to be their secret way of communicating to one another when in school. One tug indicated a positive reaction, two tugs a negative response.

On François's and Lara's behalf she welcomed all the guests and expressed how honoured she was to be their wedding celebrant. Then, pausing for a moment, she stared down at her speech, praying her love and hope and wishes for them would be adequately reflected in what she was about to say.

'When I was training to be a wedding celebrant I spoke to many friends, colleagues and family about what they felt was the key to a successful marriage. Many people cited love, respect, honesty, trust and kindness as being key. But another word was sometimes used as well, a word that intrigued me, because up until that point I hadn't thought of it as being important. And that word was hope.'

She paused and looked first at Lara and then François, swallowing against a catch in her voice. 'I was lucky enough to be present on the first night that you met. Immediately I could see how suited you were to one another, and the hope that immediately sprang between you. At first came the hope that the other person was feeling the same way, that they would call again. And as the weeks passed, the hope was that the obstacles you faced would not stand in your way—François living in Paris, Lara in the middle of exams.'

Hannah looked out towards the guests. 'What is life without hope? What is love without hope? We need hope to know and believe that everything in life passes. Hope allows us to work together through tough times, knowing there will be a brighter future. Hope makes us more resilient. Hope allows us to dream, to share a vision for the future. Hope is also vital in forgiveness. We all make mistakes in life and hope is central to us learning from that experience and allowing ourselves to move on.'

From the corner of her eye she saw Laurent shift restlessly in his seat. She willed herself not to look in his direction, but as she continued her gaze slowly drifted towards him. 'Hope is integral to daring to dream, daring to believe that the person you have fallen in love with will love you back for ever, will understand and support you, will respect your marriage, will be your partner and friend and confidant.'

She pulled her gaze away from Laurent's tight-mouthed grimace, loneliness swamping her heart like a lead weight. She focused instead on Lara and François. 'Hold tight to your love and hope in one another. With hope you'll conquer whatever troubles life will invariably throw at you. Hope will allow you to share a life that is optimistic and ambitious and fun. They say that marriage is a huge leap of faith, but I actually think marriage is the ultimate song of hope. The hope of believing in the magic of love, in trusting the other person with your heart, in daring to dream of a future together. With all of my heart I wish you a joyful future together.'

She paused. A fat tear rolled down Lara's cheek. Hannah smiled through the heavy emotion clutching at her heart when Lara tugged her earlobe once. Then, pulling herself together, she looked towards Stella. 'And now, before I conduct the exchanging of vows, Lara's sister, Stella, will read a poem that Lara and François have chosen to be part of today's celebration.'

Moving down the lawn towards the river where the wedding photographs were to be taken, Laurent smiled when his mother held back from the rest of the wedding party to wait for him.

'It was a beautiful ceremony.'

He nodded in agreement when she took his arm, trying to mask how much Hannah's speech had unsettled him. Hope. It was a concept he'd never considered before. He was an achiever, ambitious for his career. But the hope Hannah had spoken about during the ceremony, the hope of shared dreams, of trusting in others, did he possess any of that?

He and his mother walked in silence until his mother finally said, 'It's nice to finally get to meet Hannah.'

He studied his mother, wondering where this conversation was going.

'I'd like you to meet someone, marry one day too.'

Laurent stared at his mother. This chat was not following the normal pattern of their conversations, which usually revolved around business and social events and the practicalities of everyday life. They *never* spoke about anything personal. He was about to give a glib reply but the emotion of the day, seeing François so happy, recalling his conversation with Hannah last night had him ask instead, 'Why did you and Papa stay married? Why were you both so unhappy that you had affairs?'

His mother came to a stop. Stared at him with consternation. 'I'm not sure that's really a question for today.'

'Did you ever really love one another?'

His mother winced, but then, rolling her shoulders back, she answered, 'We married too young. We allowed our selfishness, our restlessness, our own insecurities and frustrations to get out of control—your father should never have taken over as CEO of the House. It didn't play to his strengths. From the first day, he struggled in the role and was deeply unhappy and overwhelmed, but he wouldn't admit to any of that. For me, it was hard to accept that the man I married wasn't the person I thought he was. I thought I was marrying an ambitious CEO when in truth I'd married a man more interested in buying and selling cars. But neither he nor I could accept that fact. We were too proud and we also felt the weight of family history and expectations. It soon became a vicious circle of us taking our disappointments, our frustration and hurt, out on one another. And on you two boys.'

Hard, confused anger rose up from deep inside him. 'When you and Papa walked out on us we never knew when you would return, or indeed if you ever intended to.'

His mother looked at him helplessly. 'I thought having one parent at home would be enough.'

He bit back a bitter laugh and shook his head in disbelief. 'And that was supposed to make up for the fact that I knew one of you was away with other people, enjoying life. At least you had the decency to only do it the once, whereas Papa must hold a world record for infidelity. Was it the same woman all of the time or do you even know?'

His mother blanched and then, looking down towards the lake where his father was talking with Lara's parents, said in a barely audible voice, 'You need to speak to your father. There are things he needs to explain to you.'

In the distance, walking in their direction from the lake, François called out, 'Mama, you are needed for the photos. You too, Laurent. And has anyone seen Hannah?'

His mother looked at him expectantly. As though waiting for a response. His gaze moved back towards the walled garden. Hannah was standing at the archway talking to an old university friend of François's from Paris. He heard her laughter and then she was waving him goodbye. She turned in Laurent's direction and even from this distance he could see her hesitate in coming down the path to join the rest of the wedding party.

He turned to his mother. His anger dimming at the plea in her eyes, at the age spots on her cheeks he was only noticing for the first time. 'You and Papa seem happy together now. Why is that?'

She gave him a regretful smile. 'With experience we have learnt not to hurt one another. Your father's pride and need to be in control is less of an issue and I've adjusted my expectations of him. He's a good man. I wish we both had been less worried about status in the past and focused on what was important—our family.'

Laurent ran a hand against the tautness in his neck. Studied his father giving directions to the photographer as to where he should position the waiting bride and groom. 'Are you certain being in control isn't still an issue for him?'

His mother laughed lightly, observing what was unfolding between his father and the harassed-looking photographer too. 'He can slip back into old habits like the rest of us sometimes.' She paused and grimaced. 'Speak to him, Laurent. Let him explain himself. He struggles knowing you have such a poor opinion of him.'

Taken aback, he stared down at his father, who was now slowly limping towards Lara's parents. He swallowed against a lump in his throat. Then, turning in Hannah's direction, he saw that she'd turned away and was walking back through the walled garden. 'I should go and tell Hannah that she's needed.'

He could tell his mother wanted to say more. But he needed to get away; he needed breathing space. And to his alarm he realised he wanted to be in Hannah's company right now. He needed her calmness, her ability to distract him from even the worst of his thoughts with her smile, her quick-witted humour.

He bolted up the path, close to breaking into a jog. Hannah was heading along the path towards the pre-dinner drinks reception on the terrace when he caught up with her. 'You're wanted for some photographs.'

She looked at him as though she didn't believe him. 'I am?'

For a moment he wondered if the small pearl earrings she was wearing would feel as smooth to his touch as her skin. And suddenly the need for lightness, to hear her reassuring laughter, grabbed him. 'You're one of the stars of today's celebrations, of course you're wanted for the photos. Especially when you are looking so beautiful.'

She eyed him suspiciously but then, with a look of curiosity, asked, 'Is everything okay? You don't seem yourself.'

She was right. But he didn't want to talk about how unsettled he felt by his conversation with his mother. 'You have that effect on me.'

She stared at him wide-eyed for a moment but then, throwing her head back in laughter, she threw her hands up. 'That's the cheesiest line I've heard in a very long time.'

She walked away from him in the direction of the river. He watched her for a moment, cursing his inability to think straight, his pulse upping a notch when he took in the sway of her hips and those much too sexy strappy sandals in the same shade as her dress that had distracted him throughout the wedding ceremony. When he caught up with her he said, 'Well done on a great job. The ceremony was excellent.'

'Even to a wedding cynic like you?'

He smiled at the scepticism in her voice. 'You don't have to personally believe in something to be able to identify brilliance.'

A hint of a smile flashed on her mouth. 'Just don't try broadcasting that to the other guests, will you?'

He swallowed a chuckle. 'Sorry about that. I hadn't realised the microphone was on.'

For a moment her gaze met his and they shared a moment of private amusement that flowed over him like calming balm.

In the distance, they could see the wedding party. François and Lara were leaning against a tree barely taking notice of the photographer, who was circling them, snapping them from every possible angle. Lara's parents and Stella were watching them, nibbling on canapés.

And then he spotted his mother and father, a distance away from the rest of the wedding party, talking intently, their bowed heads almost touching.

He came to a stop. And stared towards them.

'Something is definitely up.'

He started at Hannah's words. And was about to deny that anything was wrong, but then his mother ran a hand against his father's cheek, the tenderness of the movement catching Laurent by surprise, and without thinking he admitted, 'My mother believes that I should speak to my father about his affairs, that he needs to explain things to me.'

'You don't want to?'

'Who in their right mind would want that conversation with a parent?'

'It might ease the tension between you. It

might help you understand what happened back then. It could be your opportunity to explain how it affected you.'

She was right, but the anger inside him didn't want a rational explanation. Waving in response to the photographer's beckoning for them to join the others, he said, 'They're waiting for us.'

Shading her eyes from the glare of the sun, Hannah nodded and then, her gaze shifting towards his parents, who were now accepting glasses of champagne from a waiter, said quietly, 'They seem so close now, it's hard to believe that they both had affairs and that their relationship survived it.'

Hannah swivelled around to study him when he gave a dry laugh. With a disbelieving shake of his head, he explained, 'I was thinking that exact same thought.'

Hannah rolled her eyes. 'The synchronicity of our thinking strikes again.'

The pearly white eyeshadow on her eyelids glittered when she blinked and his heart quickened at her soft smile, at the amusement sparkling in her eyes. They used to joke when they were together about their frequent simultaneous thoughts. From wanting a glass of wine all the way to ideas in the bedroom. He breathed in at that thought, remembering that dark winter's night he'd answered his intercom close to midnight to Hannah, and as he'd gone to open the door had fantasied about her wearing nothing but her overcoat. He'd opened the door to find her wearing her killer black heels and knee-length white woollen coat. She'd walked past him, dropping her coat onto the floor, and he'd watched her walk naked up the stairs, turning once with a flirtatious smile.

With the photographer's beckoning becoming ever more frantic, he reluctantly led Hannah down towards the river.

'So, what did your mum say?'

'That their affairs stemmed from their unhappiness, primarily due to my father not coping in his role as CEO.'

'You don't sound convinced.'

He shrugged, not knowing what to think.

'Put yourself in his position. You've wanted to be CEO from a young age—how would you feel if you were now failing, realising that you weren't capable of the role?'

He let out an angry breath. 'I certainly wouldn't go and have an affair as a way of coping.'

Hannah nodded. 'No, I don't think you would either. But I think you'd struggle to accept it—just as anyone else would. I'm not saying you should forgive your father. But maybe you should try to understand him.'

He was about to argue why he should do anything of the kind, but Hannah interrupted and said, with empathy shining in her eyes, 'Not for his sake, but for yours. Don't let your parents' mistakes hold you hostage to the past.' As they neared the others Hannah said softly, 'If you want to talk later I'll be here for you.'

Aware of François's narrowed and unhappy gaze as he watched them on the path he said, 'François told me to stay away from you.'

'And Lara warned me to keep well away from you,' Hannah admitted with a grimace.

Coming to a stop, he said quietly, 'We should really listen to them.'

For a moment she looked as though she was about to agree with him, but after some consideration said, 'I think what we had between us deserves better than that. I know it's over between us and I accept that fact, but avoiding each other...' She paused and shrugged. 'It seems childish but also a disservice to how close we once were.' Reddening, she looked back down to the river. 'I don't know if that makes any sense to you.' Then nodding towards François, who was now beckoning for them to join them, she added, 'Why don't you ensure that the photographer takes a photo of your family and Lara? You can get it printed and place it in

Villa Marchand for when they come back from honeymoon.'

Nodding, he placed his hand lightly on the small of her back and together they joined the others, his plan of action to stay away from Hannah crumbling in the face of her softly spoken truth—what they had in the past, the friendship and fondness, the connection between them even now, deserved better than easy avoidance. Spending time with Hannah might be dangerous and an emotional minefield but it *was* the right thing to do.

CHAPTER SIX

WITH A DEEP SIGH, Lara stepped out of her high heels and leaned against the wall of the château. 'Do you know what this reminds me of?'

Having similarly divested herself of her own shoes, Hannah closed her eyes and lifted her face to catch the last rays of the setting sun. 'When we used to hide at the back of the school in year seven during break?'

'Exactly! Mrs Wilson was certain that we were up to no good.' With a chuckle Lara added, 'Remember how she used to try to smell our breaths to check if we'd been smoking?'

'When in reality we hid there to make up stories and games about an imaginary zoo.'

Hannah opened her eyes in time to see Lara roll hers. 'All of the other girls thought we were so dorky. I guess we were really.'

Shifting closer to Lara, Hannah rearranged some of the rosebuds that were working their way loose from Lara's fine hair and said, 'I'm guessing you refused to allow the hairdresser to use any hairspray to fix these in place?'

Lara gave Hannah a teasing smile. 'We all have to do our bit for the environment.' Both Lara and François worked for environmental agencies. They had met when François had visited Manchester to spend the weekend with an ex-colleague who now worked with Lara. In both their professional and personal lives, they were passionate about protecting the planet.

'François told me about Laurent's gift.'

Hannah's heart tightened at the emotion in Lara's voice, the tears shining in her eyes. 'Are you pleased?'

Lara gave her a beam of a smile. 'Thrilled and stunned. It has made today even more incredible. Buying our own house was always going to be a challenge on our salaries. Villa Marchand is everything I ever dreamed of in a home, even before it was renovated. I can't wait to see it later. And of course it has such special memories of our engagement. François is already thinking that we should move here permanently. I suppose we could look into the possibility of working remotely for our current employers or apply for positions in Bordeaux.'

Hannah took a step back. 'Leave England?' She tried not to show her disappointment but then blurted out, 'I'll miss you so much.'

'And me you…but flying to Bordeaux from London would almost be as quick as getting the train to Manchester.'

Lara was right, but, still feeling unsettled at losing her best friend to France, Hannah asked, 'But what's the rush. Why move now?'

'We need more room. We're only able to afford a one-bedroom apartment in Manchester at the moment.'

Hannah was about to ask why that was a problem when up until now she and François had loved their apartment in Didsbury, but then Lara gently laid her hand on her stomach.

'Oh, my God! Are you pregnant?'

Lara nodded, her cheeks flushing, her eyes sparkling with tears. 'You're the first to know. I'm only seven weeks pregnant. We've agreed to wait a little while longer before we tell others but I wanted you to know. I could never keep a secret from you, could I?'

Hannah pulled Lara in for a hug and whispered, 'I'm so, so happy for you.'

Lara, so much smaller than Hannah, dropped her forehead against Hannah's collarbone. 'Promise you'll come and visit me if we move here.'

Hannah pulled back at the doubt in Lara's voice. 'Wild horses couldn't keep me away.'

Lara grimaced. 'With Laurent being so close

by... I wasn't sure how you'd feel about visiting here.'

Hannah wasn't certain how she would feel about visiting either. The stirrings of panic shifted in her stomach as she imagined having to pretend not to be affected by Laurent time and time again. But she couldn't let Lara know any of that. Slipping back into her shoes, she indicated that they should go back to the reception. Earlier when Lara had pulled her away from the ballroom after the marathon celebration dinner, muttering that she needed some air, François had warned them to be back within ten minutes for the slideshow that Stella and their Manchester friends had compiled and which was about to show against the side wall of the château, next to the walled garden. Hannah had been as keen to escape; a three-hour meal seated at the same table as Laurent had made her decidedly jumpy and exhausted from the constant adrenaline rush that came from observing him and the moments when their gazes would meet, a pointless harpoon of desire and connection piercing her heart.

Heading down the path in the direction of the walled garden, Hannah said, 'We'd better get back to the slideshow before François sends out a search party.'

'You're spending a lot of time with Laurent today.'

Hannah felt a brief but intense burst of annoyance and then guilt at the worry in Lara's voice. 'No more so than with anyone else.'

Lara raised a disbelieving eyebrow to that.

After the official photos had been taken they had walked up to the drinks reception together and had stayed chatting, talking about work and travel. And over the long dinner, when many at their table had swapped seats to chat to others, Laurent had invited her to come over to his side of the circular table to join his conversation with Lara's mother.

'There's nothing behind it other than the fact that we still get on. I have dreams of my own to follow—you know that.'

'The move to Singapore I understand but your idea of moving to Spain doesn't make any sense. What's in Spain for you?'

Hannah laughed. 'Spanish men!'

Lara shook her head, a ghost of a smile on her lips.

'I have dreams, Lara, ones that don't contain Laurent. I'll always be fond of him. I can't switch off completely the friendship we had. Yes, he hurt me, but I have good memories too. I want to remember those, learn to have a new type of relationship with him now. I'll need to, you know that. We have years ahead of us of seeing each other, especially if you move here.'

She paused and gave Lara a reassuring smile. 'But I have moved on.'

For long seconds Lara eyed her, clearly weighing up whether she should believe her or not. Hannah forced herself to maintain her re-assuring smile, but it hurt her cheeks and her heart to do so; it was hard to smile when doubt was mocking what you were trying to convince yourself and others of.

Laurent chuckled when a baby photo of Lara popped up on the wall of the château. Her fine, wispy blonde hair was standing on end, and the writing on her mud-stained jumper—TROUBLE—was an apt description for the mischievous glint in her eyes as she lunged towards a wary sheepdog with muddy hands. And then he groaned when an unfamiliar pic-ture of himself and François in the bath ap-peared. He looked about three, François, a year old. Both of them were smiling wildly at the camera oblivious to the crowns of bath foam on their heads, which Laurent guessed, given the grin on their father's mouth as he knelt beside them supporting François with a hand against his back, he'd placed on his sons' heads.

His father looked so young, so carefree in the photo. It was hard to reconcile him with the man who had become so irritable and secretive in later years. Hannah's question as to how he would react if he wasn't capable of running the business came back to him. He stared at a new photo, this one of him pushing François in his pram, his hands barely able to reach the handles. Five previous generations of Bonneval sons had successfully run Bonneval Cognac; it undoubtedly would be hard for anyone to accept that they were the first inheritor not to be up to the role. But that didn't in any way excuse his affairs, his betrayal, his abandonment of his family.

Another photo flashed up, this time a family photo of the four of them all linking arms in front of his father's beloved Citroën Traction Avant. He glanced in the direction of his parents, who, like all of the other guests, were standing in the darkness on the lawn to watch the projection show. His mother smiled at something his father said and then they both looked in his direction. Thrown by the affection in their expressions, he studied them, his brain trying to process the easy love in the pictures being displayed on the wall and this new, calmer and contented version of his parents in comparison to the chaotic and angry people they had been when he was a teenager. His mother's smile faded.

He became aware of someone moving beside him. 'You were a beautiful family.'

He jerked at Hannah's softly spoken comment. Her attention remained on the wall, her head tilting when a video played of himself and François running through a forest, shouting to one another and then disappearing. Then there was the sound of his father's voice, playfully calling out to them, but then Laurent could hear the panic growing as he called and searched for them to no avail. The crowd tensed, as his father's panic grew. His voice became more desperate. The dense forest took on a sinister air. Laurent held his breath. Unease rippled through the guests. And then, as one, the entire crowd started when Laurent and François burst out of a heavy growth of ferns and then relieved laughter ran around the startled guests.

The video cut to one of Lara and Stella playing in the snow as toddlers.

Hannah shifted closer to him. She glanced at him, her eyes twinkling. 'Of course, you're still a beautiful family.'

He smiled at that, but then, glancing in his parents' direction, he said, 'I'm not sure you could call us a family.'

Hannah came even closer, spoke softly so only he could hear. 'I saw how upset you were when your dad was ill. How keen you were to get back here to support your mother. I know they hurt you in the past, but I also know that in your own way you love them greatly.'

Laurent gazed past Hannah to the wall, smiling automatically when Lara fell against the snowman she and Stella had been building, demolishing it completely. Stella's crying rang out while Lara lay in the snow, looking horrified at first but then rolling around in the snow chuckling to herself.

He glanced in his father's direction. Then back at Hannah. She was waiting for him to respond. He shrugged but did not look away from her. Her gaze held such a tenderness, an understanding, that he felt his heart crack open. He wanted to place his arm around her shoulders, pull her to him. Take refuge in the warmth of her body, for even a minute feel the full force of how grounded, how real he felt in her presence.

New sounds had them both look towards the château wall. Lara, aged seven or eight, dressed in pink shorts and a rainbow-coloured tee shirt, was chatting to the camera, excitedly exclaiming that they were panning for gold. The camera moved beyond Lara towards the small stream behind her, to a girl standing in the water. Hidden behind a mass of dark hair, the girl lifted a household colander out of the water. Her arms were thin, her denim shorts hanging loose on her waist. Her quietness was in stark contrast to the excitement of Lara, who was now wading into the stream with her yellow wellington boots, oblivious to the fact that she was splashing the other girl, who didn't even flinch. From behind the camera, Lara's father called, 'Any luck yet?'

The dark-haired child turned to the camera. With a start Laurent realised it was Hannah. Solemn brown eyes, much too pronounced cheekbones faced the camera and with a single shake of her head she returned to her job of sifting through the gravel in the colander.

He leant down and whispered against her ear, 'Did you find any gold?'

Her gaze held a distant haunted expression and for a moment she looked at him blankly before finally answering, 'A fake gold ring, but I saw Lara's mum plant it in the water.' She stopped and gave a faint smile. 'To this day Lara thinks we unearthed it.'

Dieu! He so badly wanted to pull her into a hug, to comfort her. A desire that became even more intense when photos of Lara and Hannah a few years older flashed on the wall, Hannah's gaze more open, her thinness no more, then them as teenagers, dressed for a night out, their make-up too extreme, their skirts much too short, but the happiness and joy in their expressions quickening his heart.

His respect, pride, admiration for her soared. She'd survived her childhood, moved beyond it, to become a warm and loving and compassionate person with a huge strength of character.

Next, photos of Lara's and then François's graduation appeared. In Lara's she was surrounded by her family and friends, including Hannah. In François's photo, however, it was just him and François. At the time, neither of them were in contact with their parents. A few years later, François had begun to have regular contact with them again, but Laurent had kept up minimal contact with them until his father's stroke.

He glanced over at his parents. Was Hannah right? Should he talk to his father? Would it backfire on him? He swallowed. The slow realisation hitting him that he was scared. Was that even the right word...? Scared seemed wrong for a grown man to use, but, yes, he was scared of once again confronting his father's disapproval and dismissive attitude to his ability to run the business. An attitude he'd been facing since the age of sixteen. He could never do well enough in his father's eyes and it tore strips off his heart.

The slideshow came to an end with a selfie

picture of Lara and François on the evening François had spontaneously asked her to marry him, sitting together in the gardens of Villa Marchand, Lara flashing her makeshift engagement ring of bound grass as proudly as she would a diamond.

Around them the guests began to move back towards the terrace and ballroom. For long seconds his and Hannah's gazes met. Something fundamental passed between them. A silent understanding. He touched his hand against hers. Skin against skin. A brief connection. He smiled at her and was rewarded with a tender smile in response.

Then he spotted François and Lara unhappily looking in their direction. Guiding Hannah towards them, he excused himself, saying he needed to play host, intending to go and speak to an old friend from Paris but instead finding himself move towards his father, who was walking back towards the ballroom alone.

The band had long stopped playing and Lara and François had left for Villa Marchand hours earlier, but Laurent and Hannah still had to encourage the small but determined group of guests intent on partying through the night into their awaiting taxis as the sun slowly rose in the August sky.

Hannah laughed when one of Lara's friends leant out of the window as his taxi pulled away and shouted merrily, '*À bientôt*, we'll see you later... I want a rematch, Laurent, and my ten euro back.'

'Remind me to lock the gates when we go inside,' Laurent said wryly.

Hannah folded her arms and gave him a pretend look of chastisement. 'That'll teach you for taking on drunk opponents when you're completely sober.'

Laurent raised his hands in exasperation. 'For the last time, I didn't take his money. Anyway, it was his idea to challenge me to a game.'

As she remembered the sight of Laurent, jacket removed, shirtsleeves rolled up with a table tennis bat in his hand, taking on opponent after opponent, his reflexes lightning sharp as he cleared the ball easily time and time again over the net, then his quiet pride at winning that was so infectious, a slow warmth spread throughout Hannah.

Arching his back as though to stretch the long night out of his spine, Laurent said, 'Time for bed, I think.'

Hannah nodded, trying not to react to the tenderness in his voice, how it added to the giddy sense of anticipation that had been slowly building inside her all night.

The dancing had taken place in the ballroom, but the wedding guests had also partied out on the terrace, where the impromptu table tennis tournament had sprung up, Laurent being crowned the overall winner as the caterers had finally taken their leave at four in the morning. It had been at that point, when she and Laurent had thought that the party was finally coming to a close, that some of the younger guests had dive-bombed into the swimming pool. She and Laurent had stood by the pool and tried to encourage them to get out, laughing between themselves at their good-natured high jinks.

Inside the hallway, Laurent closed the main door, turning the key in the lock.

'It was a great night, really fun,' she said.

He turned and studied her for a moment, his eyes holding hers fondly. 'Thanks for your help. I'm not sure how I'd have managed if you weren't here.'

It would have been so easy for Laurent to have ended the party hours ago, but seeing what fun everyone was having, François and Lara in particular, he'd asked for Hannah's assistance in extending the celebrations.

'I didn't do much.'

'You arranged for the caterers to remain here after their planned finish time to look after the guests, drove my parents home and on your return had to act as a lifeguard and fish out some guests from the swimming pool and organise for them to dry off inside.'

All night they had easily fallen into a way of managing and communicating over everything that had needed to be taken care of as the party had evolved, and for a moment Hannah was on the verge of pointing out what a good team they made, but thankfully good sense kicked in and instead she said, 'Your mum looked exhausted. I was happy to drop them both home.' Pausing, she asked, 'I saw you talking to your dad earlier. Did it go okay?'

He grinned and Hannah almost melted at the playfulness sparkling in his eyes. 'I asked him why he accepts your help and not mine.'

'And what did he say?'

Laurent crossed his arms on his chest, the teasing smile intensifying. 'That you're a whole lot prettier.'

Hannah could not help but giggle. 'I guess it was a start at least in you two talking.'

Pointing down the corridor, Laurent moved away. 'Come on, I think we both deserve a drink.'

He led her in the direction of the kitchen. Daylight was starting to flood the downstairs rooms, light birdsong filtering in from outside. As she walked by his side, lazy, happy tiredness washed over her.

'I mentioned Nicolas Couilloud's threatened price increase to him.'

Entering the kitchen, she asked, 'What did he say?'

'At first he asked me what I had done to cause the increase.'

Hannah winced. 'Oh.'

'Precisely.' He moved away from her and opened a cupboard teeming with drinking glasses. 'What would you like to drink—wine, spirits or a soda?'

Hannah shifted towards the countertop and, lifting the electric kettle, popped it under the tap to fill it. 'This time of the morning I can only face tea.'

Laurent closed the cupboard door. 'I'll join you.' Taking some teacups from a cupboard, he placed them on the countertop before leaning back against it. 'My father eventually accepted that Nicolas's increases were unwarranted. He's pretty incensed about it all.'

'So you don't think he was involved?'

'No.'

Pouring hot water into the white china teapot Laurent had placed on the countertop, Hannah asked, 'Had he any ideas on how to resolve it all?'

'He offered to talk to Nicolas. I was tempted to say no but, seeing how important it was to him to take it on, against my better judgement I agreed.'

'And his affairs, did you speak to him about those?'

'No. I'm not sure what there is to be gained.'

'I think you deserve to have your father understand what impact those years had on you.'

He just shrugged at her comment and brought the teacups over to stand beside the teapot. Hannah expected him to back away but instead he stood looking down at her. 'I never got to dance with you tonight.'

Heat exploded in her belly at his nearness and shot all the way up onto her cheeks. She looked towards the kitchen door. 'I should really go to bed. I have a busy week ahead. I need to fly to Edinburgh first thing Monday morning.'

He backed away a fraction, studied her for a moment, then, reaching for the teapot, he poured tea into the cups before passing one of them to her. 'Before you do go to bed, tell me something—the hope you spoke about yesterday during the ceremony, was that what got you through your early years?'

Thrown by his question, Hannah ran a finger around the rim of her cup before answering. 'I guess. I was very young, my memories are hazy, but I remember hoping for small things, that they wouldn't leave me alone in the house, that one day I'd be able to bring my friends from school home with me…but then I stopped going to school.'

'It kills me to hear what you went through.'

By the anguish reflected in his eyes, Hannah could see that he really meant what he'd said. She reached out, touched his forearm, her breath catching at the warmth of his skin. 'Those years were tough but then I was taken in by the most amazing parents anyone could ever wish for. I'm so grateful I had them and Cora and Emily. They taught me so much about love, about trusting in others, about being honest about my feelings and owning them.' She paused, the sudden realisation that she'd never been honest about how she felt about Laurent mocking her. But that was an act of self-preservation; surely she was right to keep those feelings to herself.

She looked out of the window over the sink and nodded towards the ceremony chairs that were stacked by the walled garden and ready to be collected later today. 'You'll be glad to get back to normal after the chaos of the past few days.' The thought of leaving pinched her heart. 'And poor Bleu must want to get home. I still feel so guilty that you had to send him away.'

'Bleu regularly stays with Phillippe when I'm travelling and he loves spending time with Phillippe's spaniels. You have no reason to feel guilty.' Pausing, he considered her for a moment before asking, 'Your fear of dogs—did something happen when you were with your birth parents?'

Her head snapped up at the perceptiveness of his question. She arched her neck and lifted her shoulders to ease out a kink, only now realising that her whole body was aching with tiredness. She wanted to go to bed. She glanced out again at the ever increasingly bright morning sky, grimacing at the realisation that she wanted to go to bed with Laurent. She wanted to lie next to him. Have him hold her. Hear his breath as he slept. She shook herself. That type of thinking was crazy.

'I don't remember exactly what happened. I just vaguely remember a man and a woman coming to the house with a dog. He was huge, dark coated. I must have gone to bed because the next thing I remember is waking to find him next to my bed growling. Every time I went to move, he growled even more, baring his teeth.' She brought her cup to the sink and rinsed it, thrown by how upset she felt. 'I have no idea how long it took for my mum to come in and find him. I tried calling but there was music playing too loudly downstairs. I tried not to cry. I thought that would only make him angrier. I remember pushing myself against the wall and pulling my duvet against myself, hoping that would protect me if he attacked.'

When Laurent came to stand beside her she gestured that she would wash his cup too. But, shaking his head, he placed the cup out of her reach and, laying his hands on her shoulders, he gently turned her around to face him.

'I wish I'd been there to protect you.'

Her heart tumbled at the intense care in his voice, emotion welled in her throat, and she blinked rapidly, trying to hold back the threatening tears. He pulled her into him, his long arms tightly wrapping around her. His body enclosed hers as though he were trying to protect her from shellfire, his shoulder tilting to form a sheltering hollow for her forehead to rest on. His hand ran along her spine, light movements that had her fall even harder against the strength and shelter of his body. She didn't fight him. Her need to have his care right now was far greater than her need to protect herself.

Fully aware of what she was doing, she pulled back, and even though her heart was racing, her voice was surprisingly calm and assured. 'I don't want to be on my own when we go upstairs.'

He studied her for a moment, as though trying to decide if he'd heard right. Then in a tender voice that had her want to cry all over again, he said, 'You know why that's not a good idea.'

'Just hold me. I want to be with you.' There was so much more she was desperate to say, to explain why she wanted to be with him—her confusing mix of elation and loneliness at seeing Lara so happy, her dread at leaving later today, all the bittersweet memories this weekend had unearthed. But she couldn't tell him any of that because to do so would expose what he meant to her.

Laurent took a step back. Dizzying disappointment crashed over her.

But then his fingers trailed softly against her cheek, his gaze moving from concern to understanding acceptance. Taking her hand in his, he led her upstairs to his bedroom. He left her staring at his king-sized antique bed, the imposing headboard and curved footboard made of wood and cane, ornate roses carved into the pale painted wood, the crisp white linen and mountain of pillows making her sway with tiredness…and the dizzying anticipation of lying there with him.

Her gaze shot to the adjoining bathroom. What if he was about to change his mind? She heard the sound of running water and then he was back out in the room with her, opening a drawer in the three-door armoire that matched his bed with the same carved roses along the woodwork and garlands on the cane. Lifting out a grey tee shirt, he handed it to her. 'The shower is running for you.'

For a moment she hesitated. Suddenly having second thoughts.

'I'm going to hold you, Hannah, be there for you. No more. I'll keep you safe, but if you want to go back to your bedroom then I'll walk you there.'

No. That was not what she wanted. She shook her head firmly and on a shaky breath turned for the bathroom. Knotting her hair up into a bun, she allowed the warm water to ease the tension in her body and wash away her racing thoughts.

When she emerged from the bathroom, he was standing in front of the bed wearing only bed shorts, running a towel through his damp hair.

'I didn't mean to throw you out of your own bathroom.'

Walking past her, he threw his towel into a linen basket. 'I used the bathroom in the guest room next door.'

She tugged unconsciously on his tee shirt she was wearing, wishing it smelled of him rather than some unfamiliar fabric conditioner. His expression tense, he went and closed the shutters of the room, plunging them into darkness. It took a few moments for her eyes to adjust enough to be able to see him remove some pillows from the bed before he came and released her hair from the band holding it up and, leading her to the bed, gestured for her to lie down. When she curled on her side, he curled in behind her, his thighs skimming against the backs of hers, his arm lying on her waist.

He whispered, '*Dors bien.* Sleep now. I'll be here.' His hand shifted up, first to skim over her arm, and then over her hair, the soft reassuring pressure, the comfort of his huge body lying next to her having her eyes droop with tiredness.

CHAPTER SEVEN

LAURENT SIGHED, DROWNING in a sea of happy confusion. He shifted his body, an unwelcome ray of awareness intruding on his dreams, telling him to fight against the bone-tired contentment that was dragging him back towards sleep and oblivion.

A deep shiver ran the length of his body as a warm weight passed over his chest. His abs contracted as the weight continued moving downwards over the band of his shorts. Adrenaline surged through his body. And then he was awake, leaping up in the bed and pulling away from Hannah.

She was awake. Just about. She considered him through drowsy eyes, her sensual smile slowly fading away.

Had she even been conscious of what she'd been doing? Of where her hand had been travelling towards? He closed his eyes for a second, trying to control the need drumming through him, trying to get his body under control. Which was nigh on impossible with Hannah lying there, looking sexy and cute and irresistible, with her huge soft brown eyes holding the same need that was pulsing through him. He tried not to stare at her pale pink lace underwear where her tee shirt had ridden up, or at the outline of her breast, a hardened nipple visible beneath the grey cotton.

He collapsed back down onto the bed, keeping a safe distance between them. He knew he should get out of the bed. But it felt as if he'd had only an hour's sleep, and in truth he wanted to lie here with her.

For long minutes they stared at one another, the quietness of the early morning, the low light in the room casting an intimate, dreamlike air to the moment.

He longed to reach out and touch his finger to her lips, plump with sleep, touch the warm silkiness of her flushed cheeks. She shifted her hips to turn fully onto her side, the tee shirt riding even further up so that the inch of lace on her hip was exposed along with the soft wave of her hip bone.

He pulled in a long deep breath as blood pounded in his ears. A year of sleeping alone, of dreaming about her, was catching up with him.

Her hand moved out, rested on the expanse of

sheet between them. Her gaze met his. 'I want to be with you.'

He sucked in some air at the soft surety of her voice. 'We can't.'

She tipped her head, her skin flushing even more. 'Are you saying you don't want me?'

He gave a disbelieving laugh, shifting fully onto his back, running a hand through his hair as he stared at the ceiling before turning his gaze back to her. He'd known when he'd taken her to his bedroom that this was the most likely outcome, but he also had wanted to lie down with her and simply hold her, have her forget all the things that she'd told him about her past. 'Nothing has changed, Hannah. I don't want to hurt you again.'

'I know all of that. But last night, when I told you that my parents taught me to be honest, I realised that I'm not being truthful with you.' She paused, bit her lip, her hand pulling down the tee shirt over her hip, covering the delicious curve of her bottom. 'I'm deeply attracted to you... I need you physically. I have no expectations or wishes or hopes other than to have sex with you.' She smiled, a beguiling smile that was both sexy and shy all at once. 'We were always great in bed together.'

He could not help but smile back. 'On that point I can't argue with you.' Taking hold of her hand, he threaded his fingers through hers. 'Are you certain this is what you want?'

'I want sex with you. Is that clear enough?'

He laughed at her teasing tone that also held a hint of frustration. 'You were never patient when it came to sex, were you?'

Her eyes lit with mischief. 'I never thought I'd complain about having too much foreplay.'

He lifted her hand and one by one kissed each finger before flipping her hand over to kiss the palm. 'You need to slow down when lovemaking, cherish every single moment.' His tongue ran a circular path around the soft skin of her palm.

With a groan she shifted onto her back, her hips wriggling against the mattress. 'But it feels like torture.'

He trailed kisses up the inside of her arm, his cheek brushing against the side of her breast, and then his mouth found her neck, her back arching as his tongue licked against the soft skin behind her ear. He moved along her jawbone and at her mouth he hovered over her parted lips, his heart tripping over at the wonder and passion and need in her gaze. 'Are you certain this is what you want?'

She made a noise of annoyance. 'Will you quit asking me that?' And then to cement her answer she wrapped her arms around his neck and pulled him down to her mouth.

His pulse rocketed, his body tightened, all thought left him as her mouth explored his with a frenzy he understood and responded to, her legs wrapping around his, her entire body moving upwards to press into his.

For a brief intoxicating moment, as he moved towards where she lay in his bed asleep, Laurent saw the long seductive length of Hannah's back, but then, as though she'd sensed his approach, she twisted from her side onto her back, pulling the sheet up. For a moment he considered giving in to the temptation of lying back down beside her and losing himself again in the cocoon of her warmth and musky scent.

He placed a teacup and a plate with a freshly baked croissant and an apple on the nightstand, smiling when she gave a faint snore. He'd never told her that she snored. For some reason he'd wanted to keep that a secret to himself. Just as he'd never told her how he'd watched her every morning before he'd left for work as she'd slept, her contented form grounding him for the day ahead, her warmth and beauty making the world a whole lot brighter before he'd even stepped out into the day.

He sat on the side of the bed, his eyes trailing

over her dark arched eyebrows, her nose twitching ever so slightly in her sleep, her cheeks still flushed from their lovemaking. He buried his head into his hands. How was he going to manage the next few hours before she left for London? When she woke, despite her insistence that she'd wanted to be with him, would she be upset, angry, regretful over their lovemaking? Would she look at him with the same hurt and bewilderment as she had in London before he'd left for France?

He inhaled a deep breath. Feeling more rattled than he'd ever been in his life. Their lovemaking earlier had been intense—a year of absence and regrets and affection all spilling out into a confusing but beautiful act of passion, connection and tenderness.

Making love with her, having spent the weekend together, the intimacy of what they had shared with one another about their pasts, all added up to the inescapable fact that today was going to be even harder than London. He needed to tread carefully, make saying goodbye as painless as possible for them both. His gaze moved back to her. Tonight he would lie here in this bed without her. He closed his eyes. Hannah leaving for London was for the best. But somehow, and he was still not sure how, he wanted to show her before she left that he cared for her even though he would never be able to give her the love and commitment she deserved.

He bowed his head for a moment, recalling his mother's shouting, his father's silence. Recalling the night he'd watched his father dump suitcase after suitcase into his car and drive away. The awkward telephone conversations in the months that had followed when he'd been at first too confused and then too angry to speak to his father, who had demanded to know if his mother was poisoning Laurent against him. And then, months later, when his father had returned to the château, his foolish, excited, naïve relief that it was all over. Only to have to endure it all again when his mother had left the following year. And then his father's frequent absences in the years that had followed when he'd left to continue his affairs. He'd stopped trusting in others, stopped allowing himself to be vulnerable by loving them. He cared for Hannah. But he could never love her.

He laid his hand on the warmth of her shoulder, his thumb stroking the oval birthmark below her collarbone. The first time they had gone sailing together, he'd seen it when she'd changed into her red swimsuit. Dumbstruck by the gorgeousness of her curvy body, he'd wanted to maraud his way down the boat to where she was sitting chatting with Lara, and throw all the other males on board who had also been staring in her direction overboard. Instead he'd bided his time, waited for Lara to invariably be drawn back to François, before he'd gone and spoken to her. Spotting her birthmark, he'd told her that it was a kiss from the gods. She'd folded her arms and looked at him suspiciously, rightly knowing that he was trying to charm her, but as she'd turned away to stare out to sea, he'd seen a smile lift on her mouth.

'Hannah, it's time to wake up.'

Her eyes drowsily opened. For a moment she gave him a contented smile, her eyes sparkling with a sexy affection that had him lower his hand from her shoulder for fear of lowering his mouth to her soft lips.

Her smile faded at his movement and she bolted upright in the bed, clasping the sheet to herself. 'What time is it?'

'It's close to ten o'clock.'

Her eyes widened. 'I didn't mean to sleep in for so long.'

'Yesterday was a long day.' He paused, cleared his throat, the remembrance of their disturbed sleep adding a husky note to his voice. 'You needed to rest.'

She dipped her head for a moment, biting her lip, and then looked back at him, the heat in her eyes having him shift on the mattress as desire surged through him.

In need of a distraction, he lifted the teacup and handed it to her. She yanked the sheet even higher against her chest and considered the cup of tea before her gaze shifted back to him. He winced at the sadness in her eyes.

But then her expression hardened. He cursed himself for wincing. He was about to make an excuse but, with a firm shake of her head, Hannah refused the tea and, yanking the sheet further up against herself, she said, 'I should go for a shower and get dressed.'

Placing the teacup back on the nightstand, thrown by the coolness in her voice, her desire to get away, he cleared his throat and said, 'About earlier—'

She interrupted him with a shove against his back, forcing him to stand. Swinging herself out of the bed, she wrapped the sheet around herself. Waddling awkwardly across the room, she said, 'There's really no need for us to talk about earlier, is there?' and gathered up her dress and shoes from where she'd placed them on a bedroom chair last night.

He watched her shuffle towards the door, yanking up the falling sheet time and time again. Her urgency, her insistence on acting all cool and calm, irrationally irritated him. And then that irritation disappeared to be replaced with an uneasy thought that maybe their love-making really didn't mean as much to her as he'd thought it did. Her words on Thursday night sounded in his brain. *'I'm over you, Laurent. I've moved on. Don't overinflate your importance in my life.'*

Following her, he called out, 'You forgot these.'

He tried to hide his amusement at her horrified expression when she spotted her lace knickers hanging from his index finger. She grabbed them from him and in the process the sheet dropped to expose a gorgeously erect dusky pink nipple. She tugged up the sheet furiously.

Dieu! He wanted to pull that bloody sheet away. Make love to her. Thick, dangerous desire was pumping through him. He stepped back. 'Wait, I'll give you my bathrobe to wear.' Seeing her reach for the door handle, he added, 'I don't want you giving my housekeeper, Marion, a heart attack by having your sheet fall down as you walk back to your room. Her heart gives her enough trouble as it is.'

In the bathroom he removed his bathrobe from the hook. Back out in the bedroom he held it out for her to put on. She dumped the items in her hands onto the floor, turning her back to him as she placed her hands into the robe sleeves. The sheet fell slowly and seductively to the floor. She tied the belt of the robe with a yank and, turning around, she lifted her own items and the sheet, which she threw in his direction. 'Yours, I believe.'

He caught the sheet, feeling more in control now that her initial icy coolness had been replaced by an air of defiance. Gesturing to the bathrobe, the arms hanging well below her fingertips, the white material swamping her frame, he shook his head. 'It's much too big for you, and I'm detecting a certain lack of gratitude in me gifting it to you.'

She eyed him cautiously. In London, they used to tease each other this way. Spring surprises on one another.

He stepped closer. 'In fact I'm having second thoughts about letting you wear it.'

Her eyebrows shot upwards. And then she was making a dash for the door.

He chased after her and wrapped his arm around her waist and lifted her off the ground.

'Laurent Bonneval, you put me down, you brute.'

He laughed and could feel her body jerk with silent laughter too.

And then rather primly she said, 'Yesterday you said you needed to work today. Please don't delay heading into the office on my account.'

He lowered her down and turned her around to face him. 'My father was right when he said as your host I should ensure that you are looked after. I've decided not to go into work today.'

She looked at him with surprise. 'Oh.'

He opened the bedroom door. 'Downstairs is in chaos thanks to the clean-up after yesterday. I have a beach house in Royan—we can go there to escape the noise. Marion is packing a picnic for us to take.'

'But my flight is at seven this evening. Do we have time?'

He nodded. 'I'll drop you straight to the airport from Royan. So bring your suitcase.'

She eyed him curiously for a moment and then with a shrug she went to pass him, but out in the corridor she turned to him. 'I want to go and see Lara before we leave for Royan. I'd like to say goodbye to her.'

'I'll ring ahead and let them know we'll call in.'

'You said yesterday that you were going to collect Bleu from Phillippe today on your way into work.'

'I'll also ring Phillippe and ask him to keep Bleu until this evening.'

She shook her head. 'No. He has been away from you for too long already. Let's collect him on the way to Royan. We can take him for a walk on the beach.'

Bleu adored the beach. And Laurent couldn't wait to see him again. But despite the determined tilt of Hannah's chin as she waited for his response the quiver in her voice told him how much of an effort it would all take. 'I'll collect him later this evening.'

Tugging the belt of the robe tighter, she grimaced and said quietly, 'I need to get over my fear of dogs. It's gone on for far too long.' Her bare feet on the marble floor of the hallway shifted and her gaze moved to a point beyond his shoulder. 'I'd like to try to spend time with Bleu...knowing that you are there.'

Without stopping to think, Laurent moved to her. Touched his hand against the soft white cotton of her bathrobe. 'In his size Bleu is intimidating, but he really is a marshmallow. My vet believes he was mistreated by his previous owner. Bleu and I have spent a lot of time with a dog trainer, training him to respond to my commands. All he wants is love and affection.'

She gave a wry chuckle. 'That sounds familiar.'

An awkward silence settled between them. Hannah's cheeks reddened. She cleared her throat, gave him a hesitant but teasing smile. 'I'll blame you, though, if Bleu tries to eat me.'

Walking back to the nightstand, he picked up the teacup and plate of food and handed them to her. 'Have something to eat and drink. We'll leave to collect Bleu as soon as you are ready so that we can make the most of the day at Royan.' He laughed lightly and added, 'And don't worry, if Bleu strays too close to you, I'll do my best musketeer impression and will protect you.'

She laughed at that. 'I'd give anything to see you wearing tights and a floppy hat while wielding a sword.' Then, sobering, she looked him directly in the eye. 'But I can protect myself. I don't need you.'

And walked away.

CHAPTER EIGHT

SHUTTING THE DOOR to her bedroom, Lara leant against it with a sigh and asked, 'What's up?'

Taking in Lara's wedding gown, hanging perfectly on a white satin clothes hanger on the door of the wardrobe, Hannah said, 'I'm guessing that you didn't drag me upstairs after all in order to hang your dress properly.'

Dropping down onto the bed, Lara answered, 'Obviously. You're jumpy and clearly upset. What's up?'

Running her hand over the delicate lace of Lara's wedding dress, Hannah shrugged, swallowing down the temptation to tell Lara the awful truth that in sleeping with Laurent she'd realised that she was still in love with him. 'I guess it's post-wedding blues. I hate the thought of going back to work tomorrow.' Turning, she gave Lara a smile. 'And I'm going to miss you while you are away on honeymoon.'

Lara shook her head and sighed. 'Guess what? I'm not buying any of that.'

Hannah rolled her eyes, trying to act non-plussed when in truth an ache was gripping her throat. Why did Lara have to be so perceptive?

For a moment she considered changing the subject but knew that Lara deserved the truth, even if she was going to go crazy about it. 'I spent the night with Laurent.'

'Hannah!'

Hannah held her hands up in admission. 'I know. But don't freak out about it. We both know that it was straightforward, uncomplicated sex.'

Lara covered her face with her hands, shaking her head in despair before saying, 'Oh, Hannah, why? Why allow yourself to get hurt again?'

Hating Lara's disappointment in her, hating just how vulnerable she felt, Hannah bit back. 'Why don't you believe me when I say I'm over him? That I have my own plans and dreams to follow?'

Anger flared in Lara's eyes. 'Because I see the way that you look at him.'

Trying not to blush or give in to the frustrated tears threatening at the backs of her eyes, Hannah snorted. 'He's a good-looking man. Of course I look at him.'

Lara stood. For long seconds she looked at

Hannah sadly. 'You're still in love with him, aren't you?'

'Do we really need to talk about this now? We should be talking about yesterday.' Forcing herself to give Lara a cheeky smile, she asked, 'So how's married life, Mrs Bonneval?'

Lara inhaled an impatient breath. 'Are you going to tell him about how you feel?'

'He doesn't want a relationship. I'm cool with that.'

Moving to the bedroom window, Lara looked out of it. Joining her, Hannah saw that she was studying Laurent and François, who were sitting at the garden table next to the river. Lara shook her head. 'I want to go down and throttle him. He shouldn't have slept with you.'

'Don't blame him. It was me who initiated it—you could say that I slept with him.'

Eyes wide, Lara turned and asked in an appalled voice, 'Why on earth did you do that?'

Hannah searched for some glib reply, but as she began to speak her voice cracked and to her horror a fat tear spilled down her cheek. Knowing her pretence was now of no use, she answered, 'Because I'm lonely...because I miss him.'

With a sigh, Lara pulled her into a hug. Then, grabbing a tissue from the dressing table, she wiped Hannah's tears and asked quietly, 'What are you going to do?'

With a wry laugh, Hannah answered, 'Get through today. Continue to pretend I have no feelings for him other than that he's a friend of sorts. And after today, go and forge a new life for myself.'

Later that morning, above the hum of the air conditioning, Bleu's snoring reverberated around Laurent's four-by-four like low rumbling thunder.

'Does he always snore like that?'

Slowing at a junction, Laurent glanced over at her. 'I think snoring is cute.'

Hannah stared at him, confused by the amusement playing out in his expression as he signalled to the right and pulled out into the heavy traffic when a gap became available. Conscious that Lara had so easily seen through her pretence, and determined not to allow Laurent to see that her heart was a mangled mess, she attempted to adopt a congenial tone. 'He certainly was happy to see you.' Folding her arms, she added, 'But I thought you said that he was well trained.'

Laurent gave a guilty chuckle. 'Usually he follows my commands.'

Reaching forward to lower the air conditioning, Hannah threw him a teasing look. 'I was just glad I was in the safety of the car when he bounded towards you. I was certain he was going to knock you over.'

He grimaced at that. 'He'll be calmer when we get to the beach house, I promise.' Then, his gaze meeting hers for a moment, he added, 'You seem to be coping with having him in the car. That's an incredible step forward for you.'

Her heart melted at the admiration and care in his voice. But she knew that she needed to maintain the nonchalance and teasing banter she had been hiding behind all day in a bid to harden herself against his effect, his ability to tear out her heart and leave her confused and vulnerable and so incredibly lonely for him even though he was sitting right next to her. How could they be so close, both physically and on a surface emotional level, but yet be so distant from one another? She hated all of this pretence and dishonesty. It wasn't who she was. Or at least trying to be. But what other option did she have? She could hardly casually drop into their conversation that she was in love with him.

Instead she turned and eyed the rear of the car where Bleu was lying in the back compartment and, thanks to her frayed nerves, gave an almost hysterical laugh. 'Coping. Are you kidding me? I'm a bag of nerves. The only reason I'm not tempted to jump out of the car is because there's a metal grid separating him from me.'

She jumped when Laurent's hand came to rest on the side of the seat, his fingers almost touching her thigh. His gaze remaining fixed on the heavy flow of traffic ahead of them, he said quietly, 'We're almost at the beach house. When we get there I'll show you into the house and then take Bleu out. You don't have to spend time with him.'

A lump formed in her throat at the understanding in his voice. She swallowed hard, knowing that she needed to toughen up, not only with Bleu but also in how she allowed his master to get to her. 'No, I meant it when I said I wanted to spend time with him.'

Laurent glanced at her. 'Are you sure?'

'I'm tired of having mini panic attacks every time I jog through Richmond Park and a dog comes near me. Last week, I actually screamed when I almost tripped over a dog no bigger than a hamster who came flying out of the high grass. He was being walked by two teenage girls who clearly thought I was crazy and ended up doubled over laughing at me.'

Laurent cleared his throat, clearly trying not to laugh at the image she'd painted. 'Okay, I can see why you want to deal with your fear.'

Turning her attention back to the passing scenery, she smiled when a golden beach and glistening sea appeared on the horizon. 'What an incredible beach. How long is it?'

'About two kilometres. *Sirocco* is moored here in Royan.' Pointing towards the far end of the beach, he added, 'You can see the marina in the distance.'

Hannah blinked away all the threatening memories that came at the mention of his yacht and the days they had spent on the Solent. 'Do you get out on *Sirocco* often?'

'Not as often as I'd like to. Work has been crazy since I got back here.'

'What about the beach house?'

He glanced at her and shrugged. 'Even less.'

'Maybe if your dad had a role in the business, even for a few hours every week, it might take the pressure off you.' Thinking about Lara's pregnancy, she added, 'Perhaps in time François might be interested in joining the business too. I'm guessing his environmental background could be of huge benefit.'

Laurent slowed and pulled off the main road into a residential street. Halfway down the street he pulled into a driveway and used a remote control to open grey panelled wooden gates. 'It's a possibility...about François. Up until now he hasn't been interested in working in the company, but his circumstances are changing.' Driving through the gates, he added wryly,

'However, I'm really not convinced about my father permanently getting involved in the business again.'

A tall cypress tree towered over the front lawn of the Malibu-style, single-storey beach house. Beyond the house Hannah caught a glimpse of the vast expanse of the beach. 'What a location.' Turning as Laurent switched off the engine, she asked, 'Did you inherit this house too?'

'No. I bought it a few years back.'

She tried to hide her surprise and hurt and said with a forced smile, 'You never mentioned that you owned a property here when we were together.'

From the rear of the vehicle, Bleu stirred, his movements rocking the car. Hannah glanced back to see him looking with adoration in Laurent's direction.

Opening the door of the car, Laurent answered, 'It didn't seem important at the time.'

'No, I don't suppose it did.'

About to get out of the car, he paused and turned back in her direction. 'This is my first time visiting the house in over five years. Only the second time since I bought it.'

Her mouth dropped open. 'Seriously?'

'It was once my family's summer home. My parents sold it over fifteen years ago. I bought it back from the family who bought it from them.'

'But why have you never used it?'

'We spent our summers here as children. Both I and François were disappointed when my parents sold it. They said at the time that they sold it because we were insisting on spending our summers in Paris. I always felt guilty about that. Five years ago, when I told my mother that I had purchased the beach house, she told me the truth about why they had sold it.'

Given the anger and pain in his expression, Hannah asked quietly, 'Which was?'

'Apparently it was here that my father lived with his mistress when he left home.'

Hannah winced. 'Oh.'

'Exactly.'

Following Laurent's lead, Hannah climbed out of the vehicle. The white walls of the house sparkled in the midday sun, the lush, well-maintained planting in the garden swaying in the light breeze. 'It doesn't look like you haven't been here in years,' she said, joining him as he walked up the gravelled path to the front door, glass panels at the side showing an open-plan living space with a huge sea-blue sofa and an off-white painted kitchen to the side, enormous windows running the length of the back wall with views over the bay.

'I've paid for it to be maintained.'

As Laurent placed a key in the lock she asked, 'Weren't you tempted to sell it?'

Laurent ran a hand against the base of his neck. She longed to reach there as she'd done countless times in London, laughing when he groaned in pleasure, the tight knot which he frequently arrived home from work with loosening under her touch. 'I thought about selling several times over the past few years but couldn't bring myself to. But if business doesn't improve I might be forced to.'

'I didn't realise things were that serious.'

He shrugged and gestured for her to enter the house and said, 'I'll let Bleu out of the car. You can wait inside here or come out and join us if you decide it's what you want to do.'

As he walked away she asked, 'Why did you decide we should come here today?'

Stopping, he turned. His dark skin glowed in contrast to the whiteness of his button-down shirt. His hair caught in the breeze and he had to smooth it down. 'I thought visiting here might be easier with you at my side.'

She stared after him when he turned away, wondering if she'd heard his gently spoken answer correctly.

For a few seconds indecision rooted her to the spot but then, seeing Laurent about to open the back door of the car, she called out and ran towards him.

Coming to a stop, she smiled at him, her heart lifting as he returned her smile even though his held an element of puzzlement. 'Thanks.'

Despite her promises to harden herself to him, the power of their earlier lovemaking, the connection, the synchronicity between them that felt so instinctive and right made what followed inevitable.

He reached for her, one hand on her waist, the other touching her cheek. He kissed her with an aching tenderness and her heart kicked both in fear and delight.

Even with his blood pounding in his ears Laurent could not ignore Bleu's barking. With a groan he pulled away from Hannah and gave her a regretful smile.

Her lips were swollen from their kiss, a deep blush on her skin.

He backed away, away from the temptation of resuming their kiss, his need for Hannah more intense now than it had ever been before.

Placing a hand on the rear door, he asked, 'Are you certain you don't want to stay inside?'

Hannah shook her head. But then stepped to the side of the vehicle as though searching for cover.

Opening the door, Laurent patted Bleu and spoke to him in a low comforting voice. Bleu's barking ceased, to be replaced with a delighted wagging of his tail.

Turning to Hannah, he gave her a triumphant smile. 'See. I told you he responds to me. You have nothing to be concerned about.'

But no sooner had he said those words than Bleu bounded out of the car, ran down the driveway and, turning in a wide arc, leapt over low hedging, before racing back towards them. Hannah yelped and ran behind him, her forehead digging into his back, her fingers coiling around the belt loops of his waistband.

A wave of protectiveness for Hannah had him shout at Bleu as he neared them. *'Non! Couche.'*

At his command Bleu came to an immediate stop, his head tilting to the side at his master's never-before-heard yell.

Reaching behind him, he took hold of Hannah's hand and, pulling her around to stand at his side, he gave Bleu a further command. *'Assieds.'*

Immediately Bleu sat.

Hannah was shaking. Placing his arm around her, he pulled her into a hug. 'Are you okay?' She nodded yes, but still she shook. He ran a hand against her hair. His own heart was pounding, the strength of his instinctive need to protect her taking him aback. Against the lemon scent of her hair he whispered, 'Wait here. I'll lead Bleu inside.'

She backed away from his hug, gave him a grateful smile that liquefied his heart and, glancing in Bleu's direction, said, 'No. I want to get closer to him.'

Admiration swelled in his chest at the determination in her voice. And then the image of Hannah as a young child curled up in bed, shaking and terrified by the snarls of a dog, had him clasp his hands tightly in rage.

He gulped down that rage and went to Bleu, whose tail swept across the driveway in large arcs of happiness when he approached, his head falling back in adoration, anticipating a rub, his brown eyes tracking every movement as though it were precious.

The rage inside him flowed away as he rubbed Bleu, his love for this animal, who had been so weak and accepting of his fate when he had found him starved and dying in the woods, rooting him to the spot. Sudden, unexpected emotion stuffed the backs of his eyes. A vulnerability, a loneliness, a bewilderment that he couldn't comprehend. Disconcerted, he tried to blink it away.

Behind him, surprisingly close, he heard Hannah's soft laugh. 'Bleu reminds me of François when he looks at Lara—complete infatuation.'

Turning, he grinned up at her. 'And I adore him.' Rubbing Bleu along the long length of his spine, he added, 'Don't I, boy? Aren't you the bravest, most lovely dog ever?'

Panting hard with happiness, Bleu rolled over onto his back, wanting his belly rubbed. Four giant legs and paws reached skywards like mini skyscrapers.

Once again Hannah giggled. 'That is the most ridiculous thing I've ever seen. You're right. He is a complete marshmallow...albeit a donkey-sized marshmallow.'

He held out his hand to her. 'Come and crouch beside me. Rub him too if you feel like it.'

With a worried look in Bleu's direction, she tentatively took Laurent's hand. She was still trembling. He gave it a little squeeze. For a moment she paused in her tentative steps towards Bleu. He inhaled a breath at the question in her gaze—can I trust in you? Instinctively he wanted to pull his hand away, tell her not to trust in him, not to invest any emotion in him, but shame and annoyance at that reaction had him smile and nod encouragingly instead.

When she was crouched at his side, she reached slowly for Bleu's belly and rubbed him with short jerky movements. Taking her hand once again in his, Laurent guided her to make longer, more soothing movements. He heard her gasp in, but then as her hand moved against Bleu time and time again and Bleu gave a comical yawn of contentment, she exhaled a long breath of relief.

'Good job.'

She smiled proudly at his praise. His heart tumbled at how her eyes were sparkling with relief and joy.

'It's hot out here.' He stood and added, 'Let's go inside. Bleu should be in the shade.'

Positioning Hannah to one side and Bleu to his other, he led them into the house. Taking Bleu immediately into the storage room to the rear of the kitchen, he plucked some beach towels out of a cupboard and made a temporary bed for Bleu while asking Hannah to find a suitable bowl in the kitchen for him to drink from.

When she appeared at the door with the bowl he nodded for her to place it by Bleu's bed. Lowering it down, she tentatively moved her hand towards Bleu's head, placing it a short distance away from where he was lying on his side curled up, ready for yet another sleep. Bleu slowly, instinctively, as though sensing Hannah's fear, nudged his nose towards her hand and sniffed it. Then withdrawing, he tucked his head down towards his chest and closed his eyes.

Hannah stood and smiled down at Bleu. 'I think I could actually fall in love with him.'

Laurent could understand the wonder in her voice. 'There's something special about him, isn't there?'

Hannah nodded and then gave him a teasing smile. 'I thought Bleu was lucky that you found him when he was so ill, but maybe you're the lucky one to find him.'

Laurent gave a low disbelieving laugh. 'I was just thinking that. These simultaneous thoughts are getting out of control.'

Hannah placed her fingertips to her temples. 'Okay, let me guess what you're now thinking.' She scrunched her face, as though deep in thought. 'You're going to suggest we go for a swim.'

'How did you know that?'

'It could be telepathy...or the fact that you're standing there holding beach towels.' Grinning, she walked out of the room. 'I'll go and fetch my bikini from my suitcase.'

Laurent knew Bleu would be comfortable in the shade of the room and, with one final pat for him, closed the door to the room gently.

After showing Hannah to a guest bedroom where she could change, he threw on swimming trunks he'd brought to the house five years ago, fetched the picnic basket from the car and then, going back into the living room, he opened the doors that led out onto the decked terrace. Stepping out, he inhaled a deep breath of sea air and turned and regarded the house. The previous owners had modernised both the interior and exterior, but the overall house structure and the sweeping views had remained the same.

The last time he'd visited the house, five years ago, he'd only stayed long enough to unpack. Unable to handle the sickening thought of his father spending all those months here when he should have been at home.

He'd driven back to the airport, not bothering to even pack his luggage, and taken the first flight back to London.

He walked to the pool, stared down at the tiled dolphin at the base, which he and François had spent endless hours racing to.

At the sound of footsteps behind him, he turned and smiled as Hannah tugged down her blue-and-white striped dress, the yellow straps of her bikini visible. She came and stood beside him. 'This view is amazing.' Then with concern she asked, 'What are you thinking about?'

He led her towards the steps down to the beach. 'I thought you were telepathic.'

From behind him, her flip-flops slapping on the concrete steps, she asked gently, 'Are you remembering your childhood here?'

He waited until they reached the beach, his bare feet sinking into the soft sand, to answer. 'Our time here was idyllic. I lost all of that when I found out about my father... He had always refused to answer my question as to where he was staying when he called home. For the past few years I've been incredibly angry with him for sullying my memories, but maybe it's time that I create new ones for this place.'

She nodded but there was a sadness to her expression that punched him in the gut. He smiled, wanting to lighten the mood, and headed in the direction of the sea. 'Starting today.'

He went further down the beach, dropped the picnic basket and blanket onto the sand.

She was still at the steps eyeing him dubiously but then walked towards him with a mischievous expression. 'So what memories will you have of today?'

He waited until she came to a stop in front of him before he answered. 'You rubbing Bleu's belly, being brave and determined.'

Something low and carnal throbbed in him when she pulled off her dress to reveal her yellow bikini. An inch of the soft flesh of her high breasts was exposed, the strings of the bottoms tied into a bow on the swell of her hips. He tucked her hair that was lifting in the breeze behind her ear. 'I'll remember also how incredibly beautiful you looked.' He lowered his head, whispered against her ear, 'I'll remember how I was woken this morning…and what followed.'

She leant into him, her breasts skimming against his chest for a much too brief second. And then she was stepping back from him, giving him a look full of bravado that didn't match the heat in her cheeks. She called to him when she was well out of his reach, pointing towards the sea. 'You can also remember how I beat you in a race to the swimming platform.'

Enjoying the sight of her running to the breaking surf, he allowed her to gain a considerable lead on him. Then, breaking into a light jog, he followed her, diving into the sea, gasping at the coldness. Out on the sea platform, he waited for her by the ladder.

When she arrived, she looked dumbfounded when he reached down to help her out. 'How on earth did you get here before me?'

He laughed and pulled her up. 'You really need to learn to swim in a straight line.'

For a while they lay in silence on the platform, staring up at the wisps of clouds that were passing overhead.

Then with a loud exhalation, Hannah admitted with a laugh, 'I'm so out of breath.'

Her chest heaved up and down and he fought the temptation to place his hand on her wet skin.

'I'll have to teach you how to sea-swim properly some time.'

'You've promised me that numerous times.' Her gaze darted away from his but he saw the disquiet that flickered there. Shielding her eyes, she added, 'Anyway, my sea-swimming is better than your tennis.'

'You beat me once.'

She grinned. 'Just saying. What height advantage do you have over me?'

'You well know that it's eight inches.'

Her eyes twinkled. 'A whole eight inches.'

And suddenly their conversation was taking on a whole different meaning. He leaned over her, deliberately being provocative, his mouth close to hers, his gaze playing with hers. 'It's what you do with those eight inches that counts.'

Her eyelids fluttered. 'Care to remind me again?'

He raised an eyebrow. 'I'm not sure that I do.'

She wriggled, her hip bumping against his belly. Her fingertips trailed over the valley between her breasts. 'Are you really certain about that?'

'I've never been able to resist you, have I?' And then his mouth was on hers, elation spreading through him at her softness, at her warmth, at her groan. His hand ran over her ribs, down over her stomach and over her hips. Her hands gripped his neck, her thumbs stroking the indent at the top of his spine.

Her body pressed upwards against his. Knowing he was about to lose control, he broke away from her mouth, groaned against her ear. 'If we don't stop we'll be arrested.'

Lying down next to her, he took hold of her hand. He could suggest that they go back to the house. Finish this off in private. But the need to do right by Hannah had him lie there beside her instead.

'Lara's so happy with Villa Marchand. It was such a thoughtful and generous present.'

He turned his head, considered her. 'I would almost swear that Lara deliberately pinched me when I hugged her goodbye earlier. Does she know about us?'

Hannah gave him a panicked and guilty look but then, with a shrug, she regained some of her composure and said, 'I told her I seduced you.'

He laughed at that. And then realised she was being serious. 'Please tell me that you didn't.'

Her answer was a smug smile.

He shook his head and something lodged in his throat when he remembered François's earlier delight whenever he looked at Lara, his buoyant mood and excitement for their honeymoon in the Galapagos Islands, how at home they both had seemed in their new house. 'Villa Marchand will be a great family home.'

Taking her hand from his, Hannah propped herself up onto her elbow. 'François told you?'

He feigned confusion. 'Told me what?'

Clearly thrown, she shrugged. 'Nothing. Forget about it.'

He frowned and asked, 'Is there something I should know?' but then, unable to stop himself, he laughed and added, 'You're so atrocious at lying.'

She gave him a playful slap on his arm. 'My parents brought me up to be honest.'

He was sorely tempted to kiss her again, run his hands over her body, but instead he admitted, 'I didn't realise how excited I'd be at the prospect of being an uncle.'

CHAPTER NINE

HANNAH COULD FEEL her pretence that she was in control and wasn't about to spew out all the thoughts and emotions crowding her brain and making her heart crumble at Laurent's words. She wanted to say that based on his love for Bleu he would make for a brilliant uncle. She wanted to point out to him that, not only would he be an incredible uncle, but, if he allowed himself, he would be an amazing father too. She turned onto her back. Closed her eyes.

She couldn't look at him today without her pulse soaring. But as her pulse soared, her heart felt as though it were slowly melting into nothing. It felt as though two beings were inhabiting her body: a physical self who was hyperaware of the chemistry spinning between them, and an emotional self, whose soul was aching with the need to connect fully with him.

Opening her eyes to the brilliant blue sky overhead, she said, 'I spoke to my parents before we left the château. They were asking about you.'

'In a good or bad way?'

'Good, of course. Why would you think otherwise?'

'I thought your parents, your family in general, might not be too happy with me.'

Despite her having invited him to visit her parents on several occasions, Laurent had always had an excuse as to why he couldn't. But six months into their relationship she'd finally persuaded him to go with her. The weekend had been a disaster. Laurent had been disengaged, his reluctance and caution around her parents totally throwing her. 'They liked you but would admit that they never really got to know you.' Pausing, she added, 'The weekend you visited them with me, you seemed uncomfortable.' She swallowed and added, 'Didn't you like them?'

He sat up and stared at her. *'Dieu!* Of course I liked them.'

Hurt and bewilderment surged inside her, some of it months old, some fresh from the past twenty-four hours. Sitting too, she asked, 'Did you think I was trying to put pressure on you by inviting you to visit my parents? Because that wasn't the case. I wanted you to get to know them because they're fantastic people…and I love them to bits.'

Closing his eyes, Laurent inhaled a breath while running his hand tiredly down over his face. 'Being with your family, seeing how you all love one another, reminded me of how fractured my own family are. Your parents are wonderful, Hannah. I just didn't want to raise their expectations in terms of where our relationship was going.'

A swell of emotion grabbed her heart. He would never really know her parents, her sisters. She breathed against the loneliness that was threatening to drown her. 'They're good people.' She shot him a meaningful look. 'They deserved better from you.'

He grimaced and then with a nod said, 'You're right. Will you pass on my apologies?'

She wanted to say that he could do so himself. But, of course, he would never see them again. Instead she asked, 'Have things improved with your family at all?'

He looked back towards the beach house. 'Not really.'

'Do you want a good relationship with them?'

'I'm not sure.'

'I think you do. I think you love them despite everything that happened.'

At that Laurent gave a disbelieving laugh. He glanced in her direction and then away. 'I don't understand love.'

Despite the heat of the day, Hannah shivered at the quiet certainty in his voice. 'You show love all of the time with your family. You've cared for and protected François since you were both teenagers. And when your parents were in crisis last year, you responded. Caring, protecting, responding to the other person, that's all love.'

He shook his head. 'You're forgetting that it was my opportunity to take over Bonneval Cognac.'

'I saw how upset you were the night your mother called to say how ill your father was. Getting to him and your mother was your priority. I bet the business didn't even enter your mind. Am I right?'

He gave a non-committal shrug. 'Perhaps.'

It felt as if an invisible wall had suddenly sprung up between them; she could feel Laurent distancing himself from her. Panic was curling inside her. She shifted around to face him directly, desperate to try to connect with him. 'There's time for you to develop a good relationship with them again.' She paused, trying to gather her breath against the hard thumping of her heart. It felt as though her body was sensing something that was about to come.

Frowning, he studied her for a long while, as though trying to understand her. An intense pain squeezed her heart at the coolness of his gaze. 'How do you manage to be so trusting of others despite everything you have gone through?' he asked.

'It's not easy. But my parents always told me that I need to be honest, to respect and own my feelings.' She stopped and gave an involuntary smile as his expression softened, but inside she was increasingly feeling vulnerable and desperate. She wanted him to understand her fully. She was so tired of pretence and hiding her true self. 'It was an important part of me coping with everything that had happened.'

His hand reached for her bent knee, his fingertip running over the faint scar there she got when she tripped over a tractor tyre in the barn one day. 'Your parents are very wise.'

'Yes, they are. But unfortunately I don't always follow their advice. Before you I was very cautious around guys. I was worried about getting things wrong. With my family, with friendships, I was okay…' she paused, not sure if she should continue, but something deep inside her was telling her to be honest with him '…but I've always been afraid of falling in love.'

A guarded expression formed in his eyes. She knew she should stop. She was only going to embarrass herself. She had worked so hard to get over him and was now about to throw all of that away. She was about to compromise all the plans she had made for an independent future. She was going to make herself vulnerable all over again. But she couldn't put a brake on the words that insisted on being spoken, how her heart wanted to have its say after months of being kept in check. 'I really, really care for you, Laurent.'

She smiled at him in hope, in embarrassment. Waited for him to say something. But instead he looked away from her, frowning. She wanted to cry. She wanted to yell at him. She twisted away from him. Willing him to say something. But they sat in silence, the happy cries from children on the beach washing over them; a swirl of embarrassed anger rose up from her very core and her heart shattered with the pain of feeling so utterly alone and disconnected from the man she was in love with.

Trying to quell the panic growing inside him, Laurent pulled in one long breath after another. He bunched his hands, self-loathing vying with his panic. 'This morning was a mistake.'

Hannah's gaze shot to his. 'That's wonderful to hear.'

He exhaled a breath at the sarcasm in her voice, his stomach churning to know he was to blame for all of this. He caught her gaze, gave her a smile of appeasement. 'You know I didn't mean it that way.'

She folded her arms. 'Do I?'

'After yesterday, we were both feeling emotional. Weddings do that type of thing to people.'

She shifted away from him, towards the edge of the platform, and gave a bitter chuckle. 'You make it sound like it was sympathy sex.'

He shook his head furiously. 'When did I say that?'

'Well, you're clearly regretting it.'

Taking in the defiant tilt of her head, the heavy emotion in her voice, the hurt in her eyes, he asked gently, his heart heavy with fear, 'Aren't you?'

For a moment her expression softened, and her gaze caught his as though pleading with him to understand. But to respond to her, to take her in his arms as he wanted to, would be cruel. He knew what Hannah was trying to say to him. She wanted more from him, from their relationship, than he could ever give.

Her expression hardened again. 'Well, I'm certainly regretting it now.'

He flinched at her hurt, her anger.

He tried to think straight, to find something to say, but his heart was pounding too hard, his brain a too-confused mess of panicked thoughts. He'd numbed his heart, his expectations, his need for love, for closeness, for trust, for comfort, so long ago, he didn't know how to open himself up to it all again...or if he ever wanted to.

'Things are never going to be right between us, are they?'

He barely heard her question, she'd spoken it so quietly. He grimaced and shook his head. Standing, she threw him an infuriated look before diving into the sea.

Hannah flicked off the shower. Towelled herself dry furiously. Yanked on her underwear and dress. She knew she needed to calm down. The anger inside her frightened her. But as hard as she tried she couldn't hold it back. It felt as though years and years of repressing herself were spilling out in Laurent's cold indifference to her telling him what he meant to her. Had he any idea how exposed, how hurt, how embarrassed she felt? Couldn't he have at least tried to meet her halfway, say something of comfort?

He was out in the living room, showered and changed, when she went there on the way out of the house.

She pulled her suitcase even closer to herself, tightening her grip on the handle. 'I've called a taxi to take me back to my car at the château. There's no need for you to take me to the airport.'

He gave her a disappointed, almost impatient look.

She gritted her teeth, telling herself to leave here with some dignity, but that pledge lasted all of five seconds because suddenly words were tumbling out of her, words that made her cringe at their neediness and bitterness, words that reminded her that she was her birth parents' child. She gestured around the room, out towards the beach. 'Why the hell did you bring me here? What was the point of all this?'

She didn't wait for him to respond but instead she paced the marble floor and continued, her hands rising to hold her head in disbelief. 'You know, you make me want to pull my hair out. You're...you're the most infuriating man.'

She came to a stop, suddenly breathless, her anger gone in those sharp words to be replaced by a tiredness, a confusion that physically hurt in her chest. 'What we have is good. Isn't it? Or is it just me being delusional?' She waited for him to respond. When he didn't she considered walking out of the door, but something was pushing her to speak from her heart, to explain her feelings and not be ashamed of them. For so long she'd been ashamed of her background, had felt sullied by it, ashamed that her classmates had known her when she had been withdrawn and terrified, ashamed of loving her parents more than her birth parents, ashamed that she was so terrified of so many things in life: dogs, loud knocks on the door, unexplained noises during the night. 'This morning, when we had sex… I saw how you looked at me. And anyway, it wasn't sex, was it? We made love, Laurent. I don't know why I'm saying all of this. I know I'm humiliating myself but I can't go around pretending that my heart isn't breaking.'

He buried his head in his hands, rubbing at his skin. When he looked back at her his expression was bewildered. 'What do you want from me, Hannah?'

Her throat closed over, her legs suddenly weak. 'For you to be honest with me.'

He walked across the room, came to a stop a few feet away. 'I'm happy with my life as it is. I can't offer you any commitment, a long-term relationship. I've always told you that.'

His voice was pained, his eyes brimming with confusion. Stupidly she wanted to cry at how alone he seemed. 'Yes, but why?'

'I don't seem to have the capacity for it.'

She laughed at that. 'That's such rubbish.'

'Okay, so we stay together. Maybe even marry, have kids. And then one day one of us grows bored, becomes disappointed in the other person. And we hurt one another.'

'Not necessarily.'

He turned from her, walked to the doors out to the terrace, stared out towards the beach before turning and asked, 'Doesn't it worry you that *both* of my parents had affairs?'

'Have you ever been unfaithful before?'

'No.'

She moved towards him, stepping onto the sea-green rug at the centre of the room, her bare calf touching against the wooden coffee table. 'Then why do you think that you'll be unfaithful in the future?'

He threw his head back and inhaled deeply. 'I've never been tested in a relationship, have I? I never dated anyone as long as I dated you. I always ended other relationships within a few months, before they got too serious.'

Thrown, she said, 'I never knew that.' Then with another disbelieving laugh she added, 'You're even more messed up than me.'

'Exactly.'

She moved towards him again and asked, 'Why are you so scared of love? What are you scared of, Laurent?'

He moved away from her, towards the kitchen counter. He opened up the picnic basket and answered, 'Nothing.'

She followed him and stood beside him. 'Not being able to love, how cynical you are over marriage because of what your parents did…it all feels like a front for something else you're hiding.'

He turned and looked at her, bewildered. 'I'm not hiding anything.'

'Maybe you're hiding it even from yourself.'

His eyes narrowed at that. 'I'm not following what—'

They both jumped at the sound of the intercom ringing.

She looked towards the front door. 'That will be my taxi.'

He pulled baguettes and cheese and ripe peaches from the basket. 'Stay. Have something to eat. I'll drive you to the airport.'

She walked away, grabbed hold of her suitcase.

He stopped her at the doorway. 'I don't want us to part like this.'

She stared into the brilliant blue eyes of the man she loved. And answered from her heart. 'I've told you my feelings…you've made it clear once again that there's no future for us.' She opened the door and, about to step into the bright light of the overhead sun, she turned and said, 'I hope you find happiness in the future. You deserve it. You just don't accept that right now.'

CHAPTER TEN

NOT FOR THE first time, Hannah looked blankly at another sales clerk in the airport duty-free who was waving a bottle of perfume and asking if she wanted to try a sample. The woman's smile faded when Hannah didn't respond. Realising how rude she must appear, Hannah took hold of the thin strip of sample paper, sniffed, made some appreciative noises before backing away. She felt numb, dumb and empty. And with hours to go before her flight, unable to read, unable to sit still, unable to bear being out in the packed waiting lounge near laughing families and excited couples, she felt as if the duty-free store and its bright colours and promises of contentment via cosmetics and alcohol and chocolate was the only place she could find refuge in.

She moved into a hidden corner that seemed forgotten by both staff and customers and vacantly inspected the stacked rows of lipsticks. She tried to read the improbable names—Moroccan Magic, Cupid's Bow, All-Nighter—but her brain soon zoned out and she stared at them vacantly.

What she wanted more than anything in the world was to be somehow magically transported back to her apartment. Back to her bedroom with the blinds pulled down.

She picked up a silver eyeshadow. Her mum would love it. Recently her mum and dad had taken up ballroom dancing and her mum liked to wear dramatic make-up for their competitions. Hannah gave a faint smile, a fresh weight of heaviness clogging her throat when she remembered the time she was home visiting for the weekend and they'd arrived back from their first ever dancing competition, proudly announcing that they had come sixth. Hannah had clapped in delight. And then her parents had laughed and admitted that there had only been six couples in their category. They hadn't cared that they had come last. For them, taking part, dancing together, was all that mattered. They had been so animated in recalling the night and some of the extremes some of the couples had gone to to psych out their competition, finishing off each other's stories and sentences without even realising it. They loved each other so much. And never took that love for granted.

Hannah popped the eyeshadow in the small

net shopping basket she'd picked up at the entrance, and realised it wasn't her apartment she'd choose to be transported to should a genie appear and grant her one wish. It was in fact her parents' house. There she might shake off the awful emptiness inside her through their calm and undemanding warmth and love. She wanted to be loved.

But she couldn't go home. Her parents, her mum especially, would notice her upset. And the last thing she wanted to do was worry her parents even more than they already were about her. They tried to hide it but even as a child she'd been aware of them studying her closer than they did Emily and Cora, more easily forgiving when she did something wrong. Now they worried over her lack of a relationship. They had never said anything but their delight and obvious relief when she'd told them that she was bringing Laurent home to meet them had said it all.

She wandered into the aftershave section. Was there something wrong with her? Was that why he couldn't love her? Was she too needy, too clingy, not pretty enough? Was it her background? Was the truth behind all his reasons for not wanting commitment the fact that he was waiting to meet someone from his own privileged background?

She eyed a familiar-shaped bottle of after-shave. Told herself to move away. But like an addict needing a hit, she lifted the lid and sprayed some onto her wrist. Closing her eyes, she inhaled the woody, musky scent. Laurent's aftershave. He never wore anything else. She blinked hard, a dense lump forming in her throat.

She didn't know what Laurent found lacking in her, but she could certainly identify one area of weakness—her judgement. How could she have allowed herself to get so tangled up with him again? She'd walked through this airport only three days ago determined that she was over him and was going to be nothing but professional and emotionally detached around him.

She'd made a complete mess of things. She moved into the alcohol section but even looking at the bottles made her queasy. Especially when she spotted the distinct blue-and-gold labels of Bonneval Cognac. She snatched her gaze away, a fresh wave of disbelief washing over her.

Had today really happened? First she'd asked him to sleep with her. Then to make love to her. Then later she'd more or less told him she loved him. Yip. Her judgement sucked.

She lingered by the confectionery section waiting for the embarrassment radiating from her cheeks to subside and trying not to give in to the temptation to buy a super-sized bar of chocolate, before approaching the checkout. Showing her boarding card to the cashier, she bought the silver eyeshadow.

She had a choice. Feel numb and dumb for the foreseeable future or try to pretend this weekend never happened. For her own sanity, she knew she needed to do the latter.

Finding a seat amongst a group of pensioners sitting at a gate displaying a Rome departure destination, she pulled out her phone and deleted Laurent's number and then, as quickly as her fingers allowed, every image of him in her picture gallery. Then, logging into the airport Wi-Fi, she began to research wedding celebrants in the Granada area of Spain.

Sitting in the boardroom of Bonneval Cognac, his father to one side, Nicolas Couilloud on the other, Laurent tried and failed to focus on the conversation of the two other men, who were arguing over the details of a five-year-old contract, which both were aggrieved about. He closed his eyes to the migraine lurking behind there.

'Laurent, is everything okay?'

He opened his eyes to Nicolas's terse question.

Nicolas sat back in his chair, a gleam entering his grey calculating eyes. 'You don't seem well. Perhaps you should leave these negotiations to your father and myself.'

He was about to answer but his father got there before him. 'Laurent is CEO now. It's he who has to finalise the contract. I'm only here to facilitate the negotiations.'

Laurent blinked, startled by his father's admission. He gave a brief nod of agreement and, for the first time in a very long time, they shared eye contact that wasn't more than a fleeting glance.

Nicolas cleared his throat. 'Has Mademoiselle McGinley returned to England? You seemed particularly close at the wedding.'

'She left two weeks ago, immediately after the wedding.'

Nicolas shrugged, gave a knowing smile. 'There's plenty more attractive women out there keen to date you.'

Though he was tempted to stand, Laurent remained seated and, folding over his notepad and shutting down his laptop, he said to Nicolas, 'Considering that you are an old family *friend*, and our businesses have worked together for the past twenty years, you will get a two per cent contract increase.'

'We need at least eight per cent,' Nicolas spluttered.

Laurent stood. 'Two per cent.'

'Antoine, you can see that Laurent's offer is unreasonable,' Nicolas said, looking in appeal towards his father.

For a moment his father hesitated, his gaze shifting between Nicolas and him, but then with a shrug towards Nicolas he said, 'Laurent is CEO.'

His migraine worsening, and wanting these negotiations over and done with once and for all, Laurent stepped forward, thrown by his anger towards Nicolas for so casually dismissing Hannah, thrown by how suddenly he didn't give a damn about the business. All he could think about was Hannah. It felt as though he were living in a cloud of guilt and panic since she'd left.

He held out his hand, forcing himself to give Nicolas a conciliatory smile. 'I look forward to continuing our good working relationship that is so mutually beneficial.'

Nicolas's jaw tightened. After a long pause, he reluctantly reached out and shook his hand.

Leaving his father and Nicolas in the boardroom to discuss a vintage car that Nicolas was trying to persuade his father to sell to him, Laurent returned to his office.

He was irritably ploughing through his emails when his father appeared a while later.

'You look as tired as I feel.'

Laurent took in his father, his lopsided smile, the walking stick he was leaning on.

'I'm glad that you're finally listening to your physio's advice and using your walking stick.'

His father made a grumbling noise. 'I've decided I must look after myself now that you need my help with the business.'

Taken aback, Laurent studied his father and then had to bite back a smile at the teasing gleam in his father's eye.

He stood and pulled his visitor chair away from his desk so that his father could easily sit, before returning to his side of the desk.

'Well negotiated,' his father said.

'If you call giving an ultimatum negotiating.'

'Sometimes people need to have things spelt out loud and clear with no ambiguity.'

Laurent chuckled at that and his heart lifted when his father joined in. He cleared his throat. 'Thanks for the support in there.'

His father's attention shifted to something outside Laurent's office window. 'You're doing a good job.' Pausing, he tipped his walking stick against the floor a couple of times. 'You were born for the role.'

Laurent stared at his father, who cleared his throat noisily. 'Your mother said that you were asking about our...hmm...about our...about how we both left home.'

'Your affairs, you mean?'

His father nodded, and shifted his gaze to a point on the opposite wall, the colour in his cheeks rising. 'I was very unhappy back then.'

Laurent was about to interject and say that he didn't want to hear his excuses, but his father's guilt-ridden and anguished gaze met his and Laurent remembered Hannah's advice that he needed to listen to and try to understand his father.

'I couldn't cope in the role of CEO. I was out of my depth. I felt deeply ashamed and a failure. I met a woman who distracted me from all of that but it was a short-lived affair.'

With an impatient exhalation, Laurent interrupted, 'Hardly. It went on for years.'

His father's cheeks darkened even further and he swallowed hard. 'The times you thought that I was away continuing my affair, I was actually in hospital being treated for depression.'

For a long while Laurent stared at his father incredulously, wondering if he had heard right. 'Why didn't you tell me?'

His father bowed his head. When he eventually looked back up he grimaced. 'I'd like to say it was only because I didn't want to worry you, but I had seen your disgust when I returned after my affair—I couldn't bear to think of you having an even lower opinion of me, so I begged your mother not to tell you.'

Laurent gave an angry laugh. 'That makes no sense. You preferred for me to think that you were having an affair rather than tell me that you were unwell?'

'I didn't want you to think that I was weak.'

'Mental illness has nothing to do with weakness. I can't believe you kept it from me, robbed me of the chance of helping you. I could have helped. I would have wanted to support you.'

His father looked at him, perplexed. 'You would?'

'Of course I would. You're my father.'

'I thought I had lost my right to expect anything of you. I had let you and François down so badly.'

Laurent nodded. 'Yes, you did...but if I had understood how much you were struggling, I would have been there for you.'

Laurent swallowed when he spotted his father quickly wiping at his eyes and, looking down, studied the wood of his desk where generations of Bonneval had worked. He stared at a long paper-thin scratch in the wood. Hannah had been right. He did need to speak to his father. He lifted his gaze to see that his father, with bowed head, was looking towards the floor, his forehead creased, and wondered at his suffering and the extremes he must have gone to, to hide his illness from François and himself. All because he had feared their reaction.

His father lifted his head and, when their gazes met, in a flash Laurent realised just how deeply he had missed his father for the past twenty years.

He rolled his neck, trying to make sense of the fact that his parents' affairs were only part of the story. It was the feeling of being abandoned and shut out that had done the real damage. They'd never spoken to him before they'd left, explained what was going on, had been vague and distant in their sparse calls home. And when they had returned, they had always been preoccupied, never there for him.

His father slid a card across the desk to him, a pastel drawing of London Bridge on the front. 'I received this card in the post yesterday morning. It's from Hannah, thanking me for taking her on a tour of the House and apologising that she didn't get to say goodbye.'

Laurent picked up the card and studied her neat handwriting. She knew all about his parents but still showed them respect. At the wedding she'd slotted into the role of co-host, seeing that he needed support. Time and time again she'd shown her care for him. *I really, really care for you.* He'd panicked at her words, at the time thinking it was because he was averse to any form of commitment, but in truth it was because he was so scared of loving someone, and for them to leave him one day. He wanted to avoid at all costs having to ever face again the same grinding emptiness, the torrent of zero self-worth, the confusion, the self-blame, the panic of his teenage years.

His gaze shot back to his father when he shifted in his seat and attempted to stand while saying, 'I'd like to go home now if that's okay with you.'

Laurent went to his side but his father insisted on standing by himself. He escorted his father down to Reception, where the company car was waiting to bring him home.

At the car, his father once again refused his assistance, but as Laurent went to close the car door, his father leant forward and held out his hand.

Laurent took hold of it, his heart pulling when his father said, 'Thank you.'

On the way back to his office, bewildered, disappointed and exhausted by his conversation with his father, Laurent wondered what had it taken Hannah, given her background, their relationship history, to be so open and forthright with him? And he'd given her nothing in response. He inhaled a long breath, remembering her last words before she'd left, wishing him happiness in the future. He'd closed down on her but she'd still found it in herself to say those words to him.

Nothing about Hannah said she'd ever hurt him.

All along he'd thought he wasn't capable of giving love when in truth it really was about him not being able to accept love.

Back in his office he realised his father had forgotten Hannah's card to him. He looked at the handwriting again, loving its precision but also the quiet flourishes at the edges of the letters that spoke of Hannah's personality. He studied the words again too, that were thoughtful and kind and generous.

He loved her.

He'd loved her for such a long time but had hidden his fears behind denial. But twice he'd rejected her. What would that have done to her? Guilt and fury towards himself twisted in his gut. And then a fresh wave of panic had him pull at his tie, open his top button. Would she ever want to talk to him again?

Given the late hour and the fact that it was the school holidays, Hannah's Friday night train ride home from work to Richmond was for once almost pleasant. She'd found a seat and the man who had come to sit next to her was absorbed by his book, no loud headphones on, no shouting down the phone.

It was the perfect space for her to daydream about her future. To weigh up the pros and cons of staying in London or moving to Singapore or Granada.

For close to two weeks now she'd been trying to focus on making a decision, but her concentration was shot and her thoughts kept wandering off into a reel of flashing memories—how Laurent had silently contemplated her as he'd rowed them to the restaurant on her first night in Cognac, him fisting his hand in the air when he'd won the table tennis tournament before running over and high-fiving her, the wonder in his voice when he'd spoken of becoming an uncle, how closed he'd been when she'd tried to tell him what he meant to her.

The train rattled past row upon row of redbrick houses, most with lights on in the downstairs rooms, given the gloom of the evening due to the low grey clouds hovering over the city.

Work were looking for an answer from her about the Singapore transfer. She had asked for a week's extension to consider it further and she needed to give them an answer on Monday. But she was finding it impossible to think straight.

The hollowness, the aimlessness, the embarrassment inside her were too overwhelming.

She stared at the light drops of rain that were starting to splatter onto the window of the carriage, her cheeks reddening with not just humiliation, but the crushing memory of trying to reach out to Laurent and be honest about her feelings for him and then the humiliating realisation that he wasn't going to respond.

She pulled her gaze away from the window and studied the page of her notebook she'd divided into three columns—her two possible new lives along with her current position.

Her current life had so many pros. She liked her team. She liked her apartment. She was well paid and respected in her profession. London was a great place to meet new men. She grimaced at that. She wasn't going near another man for a very long time. She drew a definite *X* through London. It was time she moved on. Widened her horizons. Followed a life that felt true and meaningful.

She stood as the train pulled into Richmond station. And not for the first time scanned the platform for Laurent. Which she knew was crazy but she couldn't help herself. Or help how her heart went from being positioned in her throat with keen anticipation and sank faster than a pebble in water down to her stomach when she saw that he wasn't there.

It had been their thing. The first time she'd agreed to go out for a drink with him, they had arranged to meet at seven the following Friday outside Richmond station when she would be arriving on her regular train home. But on the Thursday he'd been waiting for her, standing on the platform holding the most amazing bunch of pastel-pink-and-lemon tea roses he'd brought all of the way from his supposedly week-long trip to Paris.

He'd explained with an irresistible smile that he'd cut his trip short because he'd wanted to see her. And for the following ten months that they had dated, Hannah had never known when he would be there waiting for her, invariably with another gorgeous bunch of tea roses. And that unknown anticipation had given her days a sparkle that had had her practically bounce with good cheer through every meeting, every phone call, every mundane task of her job.

Outside the station she walked along the streets that took her home, a leaden weariness having her walk slowly despite the now persistent rain.

Stepping out onto the road to cross over to her street, she gasped at the blare of a horn and stepped back onto the footpath as a car whizzed by her, the young female driver and passenger laughing in her direction.

She stared after the car, her heart hammering, tears springing to her eyes. An elderly man stopped and asked her if she was okay and began to mutter about young troublemakers driving too fast.

She opened the communal front door to her apartment building with shaking hands. Closing it behind her, she rested against the wooden panels and resolved that, once and for all, she'd consign Laurent to the past.

Over the weekend she would make her decision on her future. And start mending her heart. She'd done it once before and could do it again.

CHAPTER ELEVEN

SLOWING TO A JOG, Laurent came alongside Bleu, who had run ahead of him and was now lying flat on the ground outside the chicken coop, staring forlornly in the direction of the hen and her chicks.

Perhaps he was being foolish but he would almost swear Bleu only wanted to hang out with them. Reaching down, he stroked his coat. 'Maybe I need to get you a companion.'

Bleu twisted his head, his gaze as ever trusting and loyal, his tail now wagging over the grass.

'Time for bed, Bleu.'

Bleu stood and, after receiving his nightly rub that included having his ears scratched, ambled off in the direction of the stables.

Inside the château Laurent eyed his phone where he had left it on the hallway table. He'd texted Hannah before he'd left work for the weekend and again an hour ago before he'd gone for his run with Bleu.

He picked up the phone, willing her to have responded to his message saying he would like to talk with her. But there was only a single message from François.

In the oppressive silence of the château he tried to control his worry and frustration. He wanted to speak to her. Now. Tell her that he was sorry, that he loved her. But he knew he needed to slow down. He had no idea of Hannah's feelings for him now. In all probability she would never want to see him again.

He should wait until the morning. Give her the night to think about his message. Some time and space would probably do him good too; he knew he loved Hannah but it felt as if part of him was still trying to play catch-up with that. For so long he'd refused to believe he'd ever allow himself to fall in love, and accepting he'd done just that wasn't proving easy to reconcile with.

He walked towards the stairs and lifted his gaze up to the domed stained-glass roof that had so entranced Hannah. Depending on the time of the day and the level of sunshine, different shades and patterns of light were reflected on the walls and the white marble treads of the stairs.

He turned back to the hall table. Picked up the phone. Found her number. Squared his shoulders and pressed the dial button.

It rang out to her voicemail. His heart pulled to hear her voice, clear with precise instructions on what details the caller should leave but also with a warmth that said you were welcome into her world.

He cleared his throat when the beep sounded, suddenly lost for words. 'Ah… *Oui...?* I left you some messages. I think we should talk. Call me back. Any time.' He was about to hang up but then blurted out, 'I'm coming to London tomorrow. I'd like to see you.'

He hung up. Travelling to London had never been his intention. He caught a glimpse of himself in the hallway mirror and was thrown by the aloneness of his reflection.

He climbed the stairs and wondered if she would respond.

Her answer was there when he got out of the shower, in a succinct text message.

I don't want to see you. There's nothing else to be said.

He rubbed a towel over his damp hair, his gaze on his bed. Hannah had been so right when she'd said that they had made love there. In truth, their intimacy had always been way more than just a physical act. It had always held a tenderness, an honesty. They had always exposed their true selves to one another during their lovemaking, but he'd been too blinkered by fear and a conviction that he was following the right path in life to recognise that.

He picked up his phone and called the executive travel agency employed by Bonneval Cognac and arranged his flights. Whether she wanted it or not, he was going to London.

Sunday morning, and Laurent's taxicab passed by the early morning joggers as he made his way towards Richmond. Once there, he rang Hannah's intercom, just as he had done endless times Saturday afternoon and evening. He held his breath, the knot of tension in his stomach tightening, willing her to answer.

But when she did answer with a hesitant, 'Hello,' he was so surprised after the frustration of yesterday that he jerked back and stared at the silver mouthpiece.

'Hello,' Hannah repeated.

'It's me.'

A long silence followed. He began to speak. 'Can I—' But the buzz of the front door opening interrupted him.

He walked past the bicycles belonging to the other tenants, stored in the hallway, and up the stairs to her first-floor apartment, remembering the time he'd carried her up to her apartment when she'd twisted her ankle one evening when stepping off a pavement wearing impossibly high heels.

She was standing at her door dressed in black yoga pants and a loose white top, a black and white sports bra visible underneath, her hair tied up in a bun, her expression and crossed arms screaming impatience and annoyance.

He paused a few feet from her, thrown at seeing her again, realising how much he'd missed her, not just during the past two weeks but for all the past year since they had split up. Yet another thing he'd deliberately blinded himself to in a bid to protect himself from ever exposing his heart to the world.

He clenched his hands, hating what an idiot he'd been.

Hannah shifted away from the doorframe she'd been leaning on, her expression growing ever more irritated.

Had he read too much into what she'd said about caring for him? What if that was all that she'd meant, that she cared for him, but she had not meant that she loved him as he'd assumed?

'Why so early?'

He tried not to recoil from her icy tone and answered, 'I called several times yesterday. I wanted to catch you before you left today.'

She didn't even try to argue that she hadn't

planned on escaping from her apartment for the day in a bid to avoid him and said instead, 'I know I could spend the next ten minutes arguing with you about why I don't want you to come in, why there's no point in us talking, but I know how stubborn you can be.' Turning, she walked into the apartment, adding, 'You can have five minutes. After that I want to get back to my yoga.'

He nodded towards the yoga mat set on the floor beneath the opened sash window, the laptop on the kitchen table, the screen on pause showing a woman reaching her arms skywards, a foot pressed against the opposite thigh. 'Is that the yoga teacher you follow?'

'Yes, Kim Ackerman.' She went and sat on the piano stool in front of her upright piano, the farthest point from him in the combined kitchen and living space. 'What do you want to talk about?'

'I'm here to apologise.'

Her jaw tightened; her eyes took on a cold glint.

When he realised she wasn't going to say anything in response, he added, 'I've missed you… and I've come to realise how much you mean to me.'

She exhaled a disbelieving breath at that.

Uncomfortable, anxiety-induced heat flamed

at the back of his neck. He wasn't sure of what to say, how to get across how he was feeling, trying to articulate it in his second language making it particularly difficult, and Hannah's cool scepticism wasn't helping either.

Thoughts rattled through his brain. In the end he decided to try to speak from his heart even though he felt like choking on the words that were so alien to him. 'You asked me at the beach house what I was so scared about. I had no idea what you were talking about. But since you left, my relationship with my father has changed, things aren't quite as tense.' He paused, gave her a wry smile. 'I listened to what you said about giving him a role in the company. He now works in an advisory position.'

Hannah's expression remained unmoved.

'We spoke about his affairs—he admitted to his first affair but I was wrong when I thought he was away having other affairs in the years that followed.'

'Where was he?'

'In hospital, receiving treatment for depression.'

Hannah gave a swift inhalation of surprise before saying, 'The poor man. That's terrible.'

'He said he didn't tell myself and François because he was ashamed. Which is bloody stupid.'

Hannah grimaced but then she regarded him

with sad compassion. 'I'm guessing that he thought he was protecting you.'

A sizeable lump of emotion lodged in his throat when he saw tears in Hannah's eyes. He swallowed hard to dislodge it before adding, 'After he told me, I realised that it wasn't just his supposed affairs that devastated me but how abandoned I felt. When François and I were younger, our family was a happy one—a normal family. But then, when my father took over the business, it all unravelled. He became short-tempered, my mother preoccupied. We stopped being a family. And then the affair happened. And François and I were left in the dark from that point forward.'

He moved towards the window, suddenly feeling extremely restless. Outside a man was pushing a lawnmower along the footpath. He turned back to Hannah, rolling his shoulders against the ache in his shoulder blades. 'I wish they had told us that he was in hospital. Things could have been so different. I'd like to think I would have understood and been supportive— between my grandfather and me we could have helped him. As a teenager I felt responsible for François. I had no one I could speak to. I hated how alone I felt, how insecure, how out of control everything around me felt. I hated that lack of stability, feeling so vulnerable.

And the constant roller coaster of my father coming and going only added to that. In truth I'm angry with both of my parents for robbing the rest of the family of the opportunity to support them, for not trusting us to care. But I can't change the past, I can only influence the present and hope for a better future for us as a family.'

Exhausted, he stopped. For long moments they stared at one another.

'Does any of this make any sense?' Then he exhaled. 'I must sound self-indulgent in everything I'm saying. I know I should have coped better in everything that happened, especially in comparison to everything that you went through.'

'Both of our backgrounds were pretty horrible. There's no point in comparing them. I'm so sorry that you were so alone back then.'

A jittery sensation ran through his legs at the compassion in her voice. 'And I'm sorry I reacted so poorly to what you said in Royan.'

Her gaze turned away from him towards her laptop screen. 'It hurt, but that's life, I guess.'

He moved across the room, coming to a stop by a low coffee table. Some pens and glue were piled neatly in a row on a dark wooden tray lying on top. 'Now, I can see how much it must have taken you to open up like that to me, given how I ended our relationship before, what you went through as a child.'

Hannah blinked. Her jaw working. 'Where's this conversation going?'

He pressed his leg against the coffee table, trying to gather his rambling thoughts and words. If any of his ex-banking colleagues who had always commended his negotiation skills saw him now they would scoff at his incompetence. He reeled back everything he'd said in his mind and then tried to answer her question as truthfully as he could, regardless of how uncomfortable it felt.

'I now realise why I was so set against relationships, against ever falling in love. It isn't because I'm cynical, or have no interest in commitment. It's because I'm terrified of loving someone and for them to leave me. Up until now I haven't wanted to give another person that power over me.'

'I'm glad you've come to that understanding.'

He looked at her blankly for a moment. '*Dieu!* I'm really messing this up.' He cleared his throat. 'What I'm trying to say…' He moved around the coffee table and sat down on the nearest chair to her. 'The reason why I am here…' He stood back up. His heart felt as if it was going into arrhythmia. He circled back to the other side of the table. 'The reason we need to talk…' He closed his eyes and blurted out, 'We need to talk because I want you to know that I love you.'

Shooting off the stool, Hannah dodged around the sofa rather than having to pass Laurent, her heart hammering. At the kitchen table she flipped down the laptop screen where Kim Ackerman, the London-based online yoga superstar, had been instructing her audience in 'inhale love, exhale love.' It seemed to be a travesty to have Kim's image in the same room as her right now, because her blood was boiling with rage. And she was scared.

Scared of believing Laurent.

She swallowed down the temptation to laugh hysterically.

He was saying what she had longed for, that he loved her. But it felt wrong. It was too late. She was moving on from him. She glanced over to the mood board she'd spent yesterday creating in a café close to Richmond Park, where she'd hidden away from Laurent having guessed rightly that he would call at her apartment even though she'd said she didn't want to talk.

She'd also guessed he would turn up today. Just not this early.

'Hannah?'

She turned to him.

'Did you hear what I said? That I love you.'

She was almost taken in by the nervousness in his voice, how drawn and pale he suddenly looked.

Not that it made him in the slightest bit unattractive. That made her even crosser. Here she was standing in some tatty old gymwear, overheating from too many down dogs and warrior poses, and he looked as if he'd stepped out of a photo shoot for how Europe's top ten eligible CEOs dressed when off-duty.

Wearing dark jeans, a white open-neck heavy cotton shirt and a zipped navy bomber jacket, he was carrying himself with his usual understated sophistication. His hair had been recently cut and she hated how it emphasised the beautiful shape of his skull, the sharpness of his jawline, the brilliance of his blue eyes.

She went and yanked up the already open sash window to its maximum opening. Turning and trying to project a semblance of calmness, she said, 'I heard you, Laurent. But quite frankly I really don't understand what you mean when you say that you love me.'

He went to answer but the anger and fear inside her had her add, 'And can I point out that you seemed to find it hard to actually tell me that—to say those words? It seemed like you were having to force yourself, so please forgive me if I don't believe you.'

He stepped back, almost losing his balance when he banged against the coffee table.

Hannah turned away and went into the kitchen. She'd been sipping on green tea before he'd arrived but now she needed coffee. And not her usual instant, but strong percolated coffee.

She bent and searched the corner cupboard for her rarely used coffee maker, refusing to speak to Laurent. He clearly thought he could waltz in here and tell her he loved her and, hey presto, all would be rosy in the garden.

No way. Not by a long shot.

Eventually she found the machine at the furthest reaches of the cupboard and, dragging it out, cursed to herself when the cord and plug dropped to the floor, the plug whacking against her bare toes.

Her mood didn't improve when Laurent came and stood beside her. He said nothing but instead watched her wash out the jug and the water reservoir and then search her freezer compartment for some ground coffee.

When she couldn't take another minute of silence she turned to him and said, 'You're welcome to leave, you know.'

'Not until I tell you why I love you.'

She tried desperately to hold on to her anger, but the softness in his voice, the sincerity in his eyes was a much too strong opponent.

Backing against the counter, she eyed him sceptically, telling herself not to fall for his easy words, not to lose herself to her lousy judgement again. She needed to protect herself.

'When we first met, I was instantly attracted to you. You're the most beautiful and beguiling woman I have ever met. You project a cool calmness, a wariness, but behind that you're gentle, kind and forgiving. At times I wanted you to dislike my parents, I wanted to feel justified in my pain, but instead, while you understood my feelings towards them, you were also non-judgemental about them. Your openness to them, and especially now that I know about my father's depression, has made me stop and realise that I need to be more understanding, to realise that I haven't walked in their shoes.' He came closer. 'There's so much more I love about you—how in tune we seem to be with one another...' he smiled '...the synchronicity of our thoughts, our shared sense of humour. With you I feel complete, whole. Without you, I feel incredibly alone and lost. The past two weeks have been horrible.'

Hannah's heart felt as though it were a lead weight in her chest—the loneliness in his voice was so real. 'What has changed, Laurent? Why are you telling me now that you love me? Why not before?'

His gaze shifted to her fridge where there were numerous photos of her holding Diana, as a newborn, in her christening gown and at her dad's birthday party last month. Something altered in his expression and when he looked back at her it was with almost a pleading look.

'When we were together in London I was still carrying the emptiness and fear that had been in me for years.' As though anticipating how she was about to argue that he'd always seemed so confident, he added, 'My confidence, my self-esteem, despite outward appearances, was terrible. I hid that fact from myself as much as everyone around me. But being back home in Cognac, knowing that I'm making a difference to the business's future, understanding my parents a little better, have all helped restore how I feel about myself. All along I thought I wasn't capable of loving other people, when in reality the issue was that I couldn't accept love. I didn't think I was worthy of it and I worried about leaving myself open to pain. But your honesty at the beach house, knowing the courage it must have taken you to tell me that you cared for me, I now appreciate how much you must have meant those words.' His hand reached out as though to touch her but then, bowing his head, he pulled it back. 'I've messed you around, Hannah. I've hurt you. I'm truly sorry that I did. You said you wanted to be honest with me and I want to reciprocate that truthfulness. The honest truth is that I love you and want to spend my life with you.'

Hannah sank against the countertop, her legs shaking. It would be so easy to tell him that she loved him too. For a moment she felt dizzy with the wonder of what would happen if she did.

But just as quickly she dismissed that thought. 'Spend your life with me—what does that mean?'

'I've been thinking about how we could make this work. I know you want to change the direction of your career. Why not come to Cognac? You could run your wedding celebrant business from there. Or even join the House—your financial expertise would be of great benefit.' He stopped and gave her a hopeful grin. 'I'd get to take you out to lunch that way, commute to work together even.'

Hannah shook her head, trying to cling to the fragile excitement she'd felt yesterday when she'd finally come to a decision on her future.

She edged past Laurent and went and grabbed the poster-sized piece of cardboard that formed her mood board for her future.

She turned it to him, propping it on the kitchen table. 'I'm moving to Spain.'

'Why Spain?'

'I contacted an established marriage celebrant business in Granada and they're looking for a business partner. It's a husband-and-wife team at the moment, and they are struggling with demand. I've found an apartment in the city to rent.'

Running a hand over the image on the mood board of the one-bedroom apartment in an old Moorish building she'd found on the internet, she added in a low voice, 'I need a new start. Put the past behind me.'

'What about us?'

She held his gaze for the longest time, seeing bewilderment and hurt and pride all play out in his expression.

She looked away, trying to control a thousand different voices and emotions flooding her brain and body and soul, and spoke straight from her heart, being honest as he'd asked her to. 'I can't trust you. I don't want my heart broken again.'

Standing outside Hannah's door, Laurent felt as if he'd stepped into a vortex about half an hour ago and had just been spat back out again. Dazed, he wondered where he would go. What he would do.

A woman approached him, the straining Labrador on a leash making a beeline for him. The woman apologised as the Labrador's paws skidded on the pavement in his attempt to get close to Laurent. Crouching down, Laurent stroked the dog, who instantly calmed. Emotion caught him in the throat. He missed Bleu. He missed Cognac. He wanted to go back there. He'd never thought he would feel this way about his birth-place.

With one final hug for the Labrador, he waved him and his owner off.

He stepped out onto the road. Looked up to the first floor, the sound of Kim Ackerman's encouraging instructions just about audible.

He closed his eyes. He'd blown it. He'd waited too long in recognising what he felt for Hannah.

He breathed against the panic churning in his stomach. What if this was it? That there was no way back from this?

Part of him wanted to walk away, the part that always believed that relationships would be toxic and painful.

But the need to have Hannah in his life was too great. The need to prove to her what she meant to him pushed him towards the train station and then into a café in central London where he plotted for the next few hours how he would get her back. He was not going home without her.

CHAPTER TWELVE

MONDAY MORNING, AND with the dawn light creeping beneath her blinds Hannah knew she should get up, do something useful, but her body felt as if it belonged to a worn-out rag doll while her mind was spinning around and around, trying to make sense of yesterday, and unfortunately she was making very little progress.

He'd said he loved her. Had even thought through a future for them together. But it had all felt too easy for her to say she believed him, say that she loved him too and attempt to live happily ever after.

As much as Hannah wished it were, life simply wasn't like that.

She'd been honest yesterday when she'd said she didn't trust him. She didn't trust him not to change his mind, to realise that in fact he'd been right all along and love and commitment weren't for him.

Her birth parents, who instinctively should have loved and cared for her, had put their addictions and needs above hers. What if Laurent's love was equally fragile and no match for what life would throw at them?

She pushed herself up and off the bed and wobbled with light-headedness. She had a presentation to give to the board of a client company today and had no idea how she was going to pull it off.

She changed into her yoga pants and top, hoping that Kim Ackerman would once again help her focus on the day ahead.

Out in the living room she flicked through Kim's online videos and with a droll sigh picked one that was called, 'Yoga for a sore heart.'

She rolled out her mat and pressed play. Five minutes into the video, her mind still refusing to calm, she jumped when the intercom rang.

It had to be Laurent. Who else would be at her door this early? She refused to answer it but after three buzzes that had her startle each time, ruining Kim's guidance to 'free your mind of all that is troubling you,' she picked up the intercom hand piece and said curtly, 'There's no point in us talking.'

A soft, familiar-sounding female voice said, 'He said you'd say something like that.'

'Who's this?'

'Hannah, it's Kim, Kim Ackerman.'

Hannah swivelled around to stare at her laptop screen where Kim was frozen in a cat pose, wondering if her mind was playing tricks on her. Running to her window, she yanked it open and stared down towards the front door.

Standing there with her sleek black hair tied back into a ponytail, a yoga mat under her arm, was Kim Ackerman.

Stunned, Hannah went back to the intercom. 'Kim…hello!' She grimaced at her overexcited fan-girl reaction that hadn't dimmed despite having spent a whole week in Kim's company in India, before asking, 'What are you doing here?'

'Laurent contacted me yesterday via my website. I don't usually do private visits but he was very persuasive.' She stopped and after a light chuckle she added in a serious tone, 'He asked me to tell you that he wants to prove how much he understands you, how sorry he is that it has taken him so long to realise how much he loves you and the pain that has caused. He wants to prove to you that you can trust him.'

Hannah shook her head and dryly responded, 'Most men send flowers.'

Kim laughed. 'I'm guessing he has a lot of apologising to do.'

And his apologising didn't stop there. No sooner had Kim left after an hour of soul-reviving yoga, when her intercom rang again. This time it was a delivery from the French bakery in Putney Heath that had been her and Laurent's favourite in London. Even with her stomach in a knot, Hannah had been unable to resist the delivery of still-warm croissants and freshly brewed coffee.

After a quick shower she'd spent the entire journey to work looking over her shoulder, wondering if Laurent was about to appear at any moment.

But later in the day, when her dad phoned her at work, she realised she need not have worried because when she had been waiting at the station for her train, Laurent had been pulling into her parents' farm in a rental car.

Apparently he'd apologised for how he'd behaved on his previous visit. And confessed that he had hurt Hannah and wanted to make amends. Her dad chuckled down the phone at that point and told her he hadn't been prepared just to take Laurent's word on this and had presented him with a pair of wellington boots and tasked him with carrying out the hardest jobs on the farm for the morning—mucking out the yard outside the milking parlour, washing down the mud-encrusted tractor, carrying endless bales of hay from the trailer into the barn.

And all the while her dad had interrogated

him, wanting to know how they could be sure he wouldn't hurt Hannah again, why he loved her and what his intentions were towards her with regards to marriage and children.

At this point Hannah closed her office door and pleaded down the phone, 'Oh, Dad, please tell me that you didn't ask him that.'

She could hear her dad's pride on the other side of the phone when he answered, 'I did. I saw how upset you were when you visited after he broke it off with you last year. I didn't say anything. I know your mother tried to ask you why you were so down but that you said that you didn't want to talk about it. And that's fair enough. Sometimes we all need space. But I tell you this, I wasn't going to let Laurent off lightly today.'

Hannah sat heavily onto her chair, glad she'd given her presentation before this bombshell had landed. 'I don't know…' She paused, feeling so lost and confused. 'I don't know what to do. I don't know if he really loves me. I love him, but I know I can't have my heart broken again.'

She heard a rustling on the line and imagined her father running his hand back and forth over the crown of his head, as was his habit when thinking things through. 'Your mother and I—' He broke away and spoke to her mother, who was obviously standing right next to him. 'Isn't that right, Jan?' Hannah could hear her mum murmur in assent. 'Your mother and I have spent the last hour since Laurent left discussing whether we should tell you that he visited us. He didn't ask us to. He said he just wanted to apologise to us and let us know how much he loves you.'

A sizeable lump formed in Hannah's throat to hear her dad say that Laurent loved her. She could hear the emotion in his voice, his concern. She squeezed her eyes shut and tried to concentrate on what her father was saying. 'I think we are good judges of character and believe he was being sincere.'

There was a shuffling on the other side of the phone and then her mum spoke. 'Follow your heart, Hannah. You'll know deep down if you can trust him. If you can love him with all your heart. Listen to your instinct. Be honest with yourself, both why you want to be with him, but also if you decide not to be with him. Is it Laurent or something inside you holding you back?'

Hannah ended the call wishing she could tap into that instinct her mother spoke about but it seemed to be encased in an ice pack of fear and doubt.

Leaving work that evening, Hannah was once again on high alert, looking out for Laurent.

Which wasn't easy considering she had to peep over the biggest bunch of pastel-pink-and-lemon tea roses she'd ever seen. She had attempted leaving them in her office but as she'd walked to the lift, Amy, one of the juniors on her team, had run after her carrying them, exclaiming with an amused laugh that she couldn't believe that Hannah had forgotten them.

Hannah had been on the verge of telling Amy to keep the flowers but their arrival had caused enough consternation; Hannah didn't need the added speculation from her team as to why she didn't want to keep them.

Taking the escalator down to the underground platforms at Liverpool Street station, Hannah stumbled as she tried to get her footing and cursed Laurent.

He wasn't going away easily.

And in the crowded tunnels she cursed him again when she was thrown endless irritable looks from her fellow commuters, who clearly weren't impressed with being whacked by a bunch of flowers.

Then beyond a group of chattering and jostling visiting students she spotted a handmade sign posted onto the tunnel wall. Written on the plain white paper in thick black marker was one word.

HANNAH

Odd.
A few feet further on, she glimpsed another sign.

I

The writing was familiar and sent a shiver of apprehension down her spine. She wanted to stop and study it but the tide of commuters carried her on to another sign.

LOVE

And then another.

YOU

And at the entrance to the platform, where the crowd thinned out, there was yet another sign.

IT'S YOU WHO BRINGS ME HAPPINESS

Popping the flowers under her arm, not caring if they got squashed, Hannah pulled down the sign and then ran back and pulled down all the others, garnering strange looks as she did so, praying all the while that none of her colleagues had seen the signs.

She was shaking when she ran back to the platform in time to squeeze onto a carriage before the doors shut.

There were no seats available so she tucked herself into a corner and studied Laurent's handwriting.

At Waterloo station, she caught her train in a daze. And when she got to Richmond she braced herself to find him standing on the platform.

But she swallowed down a gulp of disappointment with each step she took towards the exit, realising that he wasn't there.

She wanted to see him.

His signs that she'd folded and placed inside her handbag, her disappointment that he was nowhere to be seen, were thawing her numbness.

Turning into her street, she braced herself again, her gaze shooting towards the front door of her house. But there was no sign of him.

Inside her apartment she crowded the tea roses into the three vases she owned and had no choice but to place the remaining flowers into a drinking glass.

She changed into her black jeans and a sleeveless white lace top and waited for him to ring her intercom.

An hour later she was angry and cross. What was he playing at?

By nine o'clock she was a bundle of nerves. Had something happened to him? She pictured him lying on a hospital trolley.

She picked up her phone. She needed to call him, make sure he was okay. She yelped when her intercom rang.

She picked up the hand piece. 'What the hell are you playing at, Laurent?'

A young hesitant male voice answered, 'Is that Hannah McGinley? I've a package for you.'

Hannah ran down the stairs and apologised to the startled-looking delivery driver, who handed her a poster-sized package and legged it back to his van.

Upstairs Hannah pulled off the plain brown paper wrapping to find a mood board beneath. She stared at the images on it, trying to understand what they all meant, a giddiness, a disbelief fizzing through her bloodstream. She gave a little cry when she spotted at the centre of the board a photograph of herself and Laurent high-fiving each other at Lara's wedding. Her breath caught at the shared affection and familiarity in which they were smiling at one another, at how unbearably handsome Laurent looked with his shirtsleeves rolled up, evening shadow adding to his dark looks.

She stared at the board, guessing what each photo and carefully written word might mean, desperate to hear Laurent's explanation.

She picked up her phone, realising he was going to wait for her to contact him.

He was waiting to see if she would trust and believe him when he said he loved her.

A hand resting on her stomach, she closed her eyes and listened to her instinct.

Then she rang his number. When he answered she struggled to speak, completely overwhelmed by how tenderly, how nervously he said her name.

Eventually she managed to ask, 'Where are you?'

'I can be with you within half an hour.'

Hannah sighed out her answer—'Good!'—and hung up.

Laurent willed the taxi driver to drive faster but knew that they were already at the upper speed limits.

Hannah had sounded upset on the phone.

What was he facing?

He lowered his window, needing some air.

When he arrived at her apartment she buzzed him up without him even having to press the intercom button.

He took the stairs slowly, dreading what might come.

She was at her door waiting for him and with an uncertain smile turned and led him inside.

It was only when she lifted the mood board he had delivered to her, and he saw how her hands were shaking, that he realised that she was as nervous as he was.

'Will you explain what all these images mean?'

He gave her a self-deprecatory smile. 'Given how poorly I managed to explain myself verbally yesterday, I decided to follow your lead and show you in images the future I dream of for us both.'

Taking hold of the board, he pointed to the various travel images on the top right-hand corner. 'These are the places I want to visit with you. Costa Rica, Whistler, St Petersburg...' Pausing to point to one image in particular, he added, 'The Soap Museum in Antwerp.'

He was gifted with an amused smile from Hannah and, taking courage from it, pointed to the image of four children on a beach, all looking cute but mutinous, their dark hair ruffled, clearly not impressed to have been forced to stop digging an enormous hole in the sand. 'These four represent the children I want us to have, strong, independent, spirited children.'

With trembling fingers she tucked a strand

of her loose hair behind her ear and nodded for him to continue, her eyes bright, her cheeks flushed.

'And this couple, celebrating their fifth wedding anniversary with friends and family, I want that to be us. But of course we will be having champagne and brandy cocktails.'

Touching the photo of the children, Hannah said, 'Kim Ackerman, the croissants, the flowers, the signs, this board…are all incredible, but what means the most to me is that you went and visited my parents.'

He swallowed at the raw vulnerable emotion in her voice, felt his heart about give way with the tension of it all. 'Your parents deserved my apology. And I needed to show you how much I love you.'

She took the mood board from his grasp and placed it down on the table. Then, coming in front of him, she stared up into his eyes, as though she was trying to fully know him. 'You do love me, don't you?'

It wasn't a question but more a statement of wonder.

He wanted to reach out and touch her. But he stayed where he was, instinctively knowing he needed to give her space. 'I realised I loved you one evening when waiting for you at Richmond station. Your smile when you got off your train and saw me lit a fire of happiness in me that was extraordinary in its power but also terrifying.' He heard his voice crack and paused in a bid to gather himself before admitting, 'I was terrified of loving you and being hurt.'

She stepped towards him, her bare toes curling over the tops of his shoes. Her hand reached for his cheek; he closed his eyes at how tender her touch was. 'I will never hurt you.'

He opened his eyes and said the most honest words he'd ever spoken. 'I know you won't.'

He touched her cheek, their gazes holding, holding, holding, silently communicating the wonder, the beauty, the hope of this moment. Then he gently kissed her, his heart aching with the honesty between them, his bones dissolving at the sensation of being in the place where you belonged, where you could be the true version of yourself.

Reluctantly he pulled back, knowing they still had things to discuss.

Taking her by the hand, he led her over to the sofa. When they were both seated, angled into one another, he asked, 'Have you decided what you are going to do work-wise in the future?'

Hannah nodded. 'I told my senior partner that I'm leaving today.'

Laurent flinched. 'Are you still going to Granada?'

She dipped her head for a moment. He braced himself. She hadn't actually told him her feelings for him yet. She had never said that she loved him. When she looked back up, she tilted her head, gave him a shy smile. 'There's a château in Cognac that sounds more appealing.'

He grinned at that but then, shuffling on the sofa, he said quietly, 'I love you...but I still don't know how you feel about me.'

Hannah stared at him, perplexed, and then she started giggling. 'I love you, of course! How could you not know that?' Lifting a pillow, she hit him with it playfully. 'I love you, Laurent Bonneval. I love your loyalty to François, to your parents, to your family business. I love your kindness, your ability to read my mind, I love how sexy you look twenty-four-seven and I love the future you have mapped out for us. I love everything about you and will even tolerate the smelliest of cheeses in our fridge.'

Laurent grinned and grinned and then, placing a tender kiss on her forehead, he knelt before her.

Hannah paled.

He cleared his throat, suddenly really nervous again. 'I want to ask you something but I'm not sure if it's too early.'

Her eyes were glistening with tears. 'I'm not

going to change my mind about anything. I love you and want to move to be with you in Cognac.'

'I spoke to your dad today, got his permission.'

At that a tear dropped onto Hannah's cheek. 'You did?'

'And when I got back to London this afternoon I went shopping.'

Hannah gasped when he took a pale blue box from his blazer jacket. Holding it out towards her, he said with the honesty that he wanted to be the trademark of their marriage, 'I'm still not sure I fully understand love, but I'm going to stop trying to understand it and just believe in it instead.' Opening up the ring box, he held his breath as Hannah stared at the five-stone diamond ring.

'It's so beautiful.'

He grinned at her softly spoken awe and, taking the ring out of the box, he took hold of her hand and asked, 'Hannah, will you be my wife?'

Hannah nodded, laughed, wiped away a tear from her cheek, laughed again, made a funny exclamation noise when he placed the ring on her finger and then grinned and grinned at him, her hands flapping in excitement.

And when she calmed, she edged forward on the sofa, her hands capturing his face, her nose touching his. 'I will love you for ever and ever, Laurent.'

EPILOGUE

It was a tricky manoeuvre, getting the full skirt of her wedding gown down the narrow steps of the farmhouse while carrying a heavy train. Hannah knew she could call for help but preferred to let her family and Lara chat and lark about in the kitchen instead.

At the bottom of the stairs, she paused to gather her breath and smiled at the consternation coming from the kitchen. Her mum and dad were arguing over how he should correctly knot his bow tie, Cora was pleading with her husband to stop Diana, who was now an adventurous fifteen-month-old, from crawling along the floor and Lara was cooing to her three-month-old daughter, Ruth.

Laurent had been right after all when he'd insisted that their wedding blessing take place on her parents' farm. At first Hannah had said no, that the château was a more suitable venue. Not only because of its size and facilities but also because it was the place where day by day they were becoming ever closer, where laughter rang out during their long weekend lunches with family and friends, where Hannah got to study Laurent and wonder at the security, the grounding, the absolute peace his love brought to her.

Now, though, she could see that the farm was the perfect place for them to marry. This house, so full of warmth and love, had been integral in nursing the terrified child she once had been.

They had officially married earlier in the week at a low-key but deeply intimate civil ceremony in Cognac Town Hall before making the journey to England.

She listened to all the voices in the kitchen, all the people she loved so dearly, tears filling her eyes at the knowledge that their marriage was soon going to be blessed in their presence.

She was excited, nervous and ever so slightly dazed.

But most of all she was grateful. Grateful that both she and Laurent had been able to deal with their pasts and focus on the future. Grateful that they had found one another. Grateful that they were surrounded by so much love and positivity and hope. She was grateful for Laurent's love, his daily kindness and unwavering support as she established her celebrant business, his loyalty, his determination to create and maintain a strong and honest marriage.

Hannah smiled when Lara opened the kitchen door. Ruth, wearing a lilac dress in the same shade as her mum's, was asleep in her arms. Lara along with Emily and Cora were her bridesmaids today, Diana her flower girl.

Lara gave a gasp. 'Oh, Hannah, I'm going to cry. You look so beautiful.'

A rush from the kitchen ensued and Hannah giggled at all the excited exclamations.

Coming towards her, tears in his eyes, her father passed her bouquet of irises to her. The flowers of hope.

And then they were all on the way out through the front walled garden, passing by the meadow with views out to the green valley beyond, and around to the terraced garden to the side of the house, her mum's pride and joy, the borders surrounding the cricket-pitch-worthy lawn abundant with clematises, pastel tea roses, lilies and alliums.

Her heart kicked hard when she saw Laurent standing in front of the seated guests.

Gripping her dad's arm even tighter, she walked towards him, her heart brimming with love and hope.

When Cora and Diana reached him, Laurent scooped Diana up and pecked her affectionately on the cheek. Diana's giggles ran across the entire terrace and the guests laughed in response and suddenly the suspenseful tension of the day was gone.

And when Lara arrived at the top of the aisle, Laurent gently touched his hand against one of Ruth's tiny lilac socks and smiled in delight and pride at his niece.

And then it was her turn.

His brilliant blue gaze enveloped her.

She moved towards him, the momentous significance of declaring their love publicly causing a tear to float down her cheek.

Laurent hugged her father.

And then he was smiling down at her, his eyes reflecting her own nervousness and amazement, and then he pulled her into him.

'Don't cry,' he whispered against her ear.

She pulled back a fraction. Gave a little hiccup. 'It's my hormones.'

Laurent frowned and then his mouth dropped open. 'Are you…?'

Nodding, she whispered against his ear, her heart kicking at the security, the sense of peace that she found standing so close to him. 'Pregnant. Yes.'

His eyes dancing with wonder, he captured her face between his hands, was about to kiss her until Jamie, their wedding celebrant and a friend of Hannah's, cleared his throat loudly and said cheerfully, 'That's for later, folks.'

They grinned at one another and turned towards Jamie, Laurent lacing his fingers through hers.

Hannah turned for a moment to her family. She smiled at her dad and then looked at her mum, who gave her a knowing smile and nod that said that now Hannah was living life as it should be—trusting and hoping and loving and being honest with yourself.

She turned back to Laurent.

He dipped his head and said softly, 'I will treasure you, our baby, and every day of our marriage.'

* * * * *

*If you enjoyed this story,
check out these other great reads
from Katrina Cudmore*

Resisting the Italian Single Dad
Christmas with Her Duke
Tempted by Her Greek Tycoon
Their Baby Surprise

All available now!